THE **BEST MONEY**
MURDER CAN BUY

A Stokes Moran Mystery

NEIL McGAUGHEY

SCRIBNER

SCRIBNER
1230 Avenue of the Americas
New York, NY 10020

SCRIBNER and design are registered trademarks of Simon & Schuster Inc.

Manufactured in the United States of America

Text set in Bauer Bodoni

1 3 5 7 9 10 8 6 4 2

Library of Congress Cataloging-in-Publication Data
McGaughey, Neil.
The best money murder can buy/Neil McGaughey.
p. cm.
I. Title.
PS3563.C36372B47   1996
813'.54—dc20
95–26791
CIP

ISBN 0-684-19761-8

For my grandmother

Dora Daughdrill Bridges
1898 — 1985

With all my love

ACKNOWLEDGMENTS

Once again I would like to thank Nolan and Nancy Minton for walking with me every step of the way; Kathie Adams, Lynn Clark, Sue Hathorn, Jane Lee, Mark Smith, and Shirley Tipton for their constant encouragement; Orley Hood and the *Clarion-Ledger* for their continued support; fellow writers Nevada Barr, Sophie Dunbar, Earlene Fowler, and Charles Wilson for their friendship; and Susanne Kirk, my editor at Scribner, and Martha Kaplan, my agent, for their intrinsic contributions.

As always, I would like to express a special and continued indebtedness to Don.

Lastly, I wish to acknowledge the irreplaceable loss in my life of a wonderful Irish setter named Boo. A loyal and constant companion for almost twelve years, she will never be forgotten. Thankfully, in the character of Bootsie, her spirit lives on in these pages.

THE BEST MONEY
MURDER CAN BUY

CHAPTER 1

*"Like a charging bull
elephant,
this novel gored me
with its
wonderful opening line
and never let go."*

—Stokes Moran,

on Karin McQuillan's *Elephants' Graveyard*

"*T*he hell with it!"

I slammed the receiver down. Lee, sitting comfortably on the sofa with my dog Bootsie nestled snugly around her feet, glared accusingly at me over the top of her magazine. I noticed it was *Better Homes & Gardens*—an unusual choice for my normally *Vanity Fair* wife.

"Careful you don't break the furniture, Kyle," she warned sarcastically.

"They put me on terminal hold again," I said, ignoring her gibe. "You wouldn't see them treating Anthony Boucher like this," I complained as I plopped down on the couch next to Lee.

11

"No," she agreed, "you wouldn't. For one thing, Boucher's no longer among the living," she deadpanned, "and, for another, even if he were alive, I'm sure he'd have enough sense not to persist in identifying himself as William Anthony Parker White."

"But that was his real name," I argued.

"But everyone knew him as Anthony Boucher, the mystery critic for *The New York Times*." Lee turned toward me, her eyes holding a smile. "Just as everyone knows you as Stokes Moran."

I continued to sulk. "I signed the contracts as Kyle Malachi. You'd think my publisher would eventually put the two together."

Lee sighed. "Why don't you just say it's Stokes Moran calling? That would simplify it for everybody, and it would keep you from getting mad all the time."

I stood up. "Because it's not my real name. Stokes Moran is a pseudonym I created strictly for my mystery reviews. It's not who I am."

"But it's how you are known." Lee slapped the magazine down on top of the coffee table. "And it's how you got this book contract in the first place." She moved her legs, momentarily dislodging the slumbering Irish setter from around her feet. "I don't understand your growing animosity with the Moran name."

I started to respond, then abruptly stopped. How could I explain feelings I didn't fully understand myself? I had invented Stokes Moran, had devoted my time and energies in establishing the name's credibility, and had lived harmoniously with the dual identity for several years. Why now, when I stood poised on the threshold of major success—the Christmas hardcover publication of a collection of reviews, essays, and lists under the admittedly self-revealing title *Alias Stokes Moran*—was I suddenly balking at the attention the pseudonym was getting? Could it possibly be that I was envious or jealous of my own creation?

"I think you're jealous of Moran," Lee said, echoing my own thoughts.

"That's ridiculous."

"Oh, is it?" she asked, rising to her feet. "Then how do you explain your obvious anger these days whenever Moran's name is mentioned?"

"It's not anger."

Lee arched her eyebrows, conveying a somewhat dubious consternation. "Then just exactly what would you call it?"

"I don't know." I rubbed my hands through my hair. "Friendly rivalry," I finally offered.

My wife laughed. "That's a good one," she said. I smiled back. Lee had a knack for kidding me out of bad moods and ill tempers. I hated to admit it, but she knew me better than anyone, perhaps even better than I knew myself. Somehow, through our easy acceptance of each other, we had gone from newlyweds to an old married couple in only a short three months.

Since February 17, the day Lee and I had officially tied the knot, both of us had made necessary adjustments in our ways of life. Each of us had lived alone for many years—Lee, happily ensconced with her client list in her Manhattan apartment, firmly established in her career as a big-time literary agent—and me, blithely unaware of the world beyond the walls of my

Tipton, Connecticut, hideaway and yet perfectly settled in a closed world of constant mystery novels and frequent dog antics. It's a wonder Lee and I ever got together at all.

But we did, and the past ninety days had proved just how much we were suited to each other. While Lee operated out of her New York City address three days a week, I maximized the remainder of my self-imposed sabbatical from mystery reviewing. The previous October, I had managed to stockpile a six-month supply of reviews so that I could devote my full attention to the writing of my own mystery novel, but, fairly early in the process, my best efforts had been interrupted on a couple of occasions by some unexpected occurrences. For the past several weeks, though, my progress had been virtually unimpeded, and I was now at the point of glimpsing the finish. Which was most welcome, since my backlog of reviews had run out. For several days now, I had nervously anticipated the inevitable necessity of reading and reviewing a mystery novel simultaneous with the writing of one. The attempt to concurrently fill these two most different roles presented a potentially confusing dichotomy I did not especially relish and had studiously tried to avoid.

But, like death and taxes, the moment had invariably arrived. At this very minute, dust jacket safely removed, Sue Grafton's latest alphabet thriller lay virgin on my nightstand, ready for me to once again begin the weekly grind of satisfying my voracious syndicated public—a public which, with the attendant publicity surrounding the forthcoming publication of *Alias Stokes Moran*, had grown to a weekly subscription of one hundred and twenty-two newspapers, Sunday supplements, and mystery fanzines in forty-two states. As

Lee, in this instance more agent than wife, had gleefully crowed, "You are definitely hot." On second thought, maybe Lee had made that claim when she was in a more wifely mode. But either way, one thing was certain—I was currently enjoying the greatest success of my adult life.

Or, rather, Stokes Moran was.

Even after Lee's as usual on-the-mark analysis as well as my own emotional gut check, I still couldn't rid myself of what I knew was clearly an unreasonable resentment toward my alter identity. I supposed it was something best ignored, something best left alone.

"I'm hungry," I suddenly announced.

"There's some tuna casserole left over from dinner," Lee answered, once again engrossed behind the pages of another magazine. This time it was *House Beautiful*. Was my worldly wife suddenly going domestic on me? This, I decided, was a development that definitely deserved further investigation.

"Do you want me to heat some up for you too?" I asked, heading toward the kitchen. I glanced back, heard Lee's "No, thank you," and watched Bootsie climb determinedly to her feet. My dog's built-in food radar never failed her. By the time I placed the cold dish inside the microwave, programmed the timer for a hundred and twenty seconds, and hit the power button, Bootsie was already standing at my side, wagging her tail encouragingly.

"Not so fast," I cautioned her. "It's got to warm up first."

With the soft humming of the oven as a backdrop, I pulled open a drawer and lifted out a spoon. I impatiently tapped the edge of the spoon on the metal handle of the microwave and watched the numbers count down. Finally—five, four, three, two, one. The high-pitched beep told me what I already knew. I reached for an oven mitt, opened the microwave's door, and lifted out the hot dish.

"Yuk," I commented to Bootsie, who all this time had been waiting much more patiently than her master. "It looks like you might get more of this than usual." The dog started to dance around excitedly. I frowned down at her, shaking my head sympathetically. "You don't know what it is you're letting yourself in for."

I placed the dish on one of the cold burners of the stove and lifted off the lid. Compressed air, as hot as the breath of a ancient dragon and smelling worse, singed my nose and made my eyes water. I dipped in the spoon and slowly stirred the contents. Gradually, the totally unappetizing congealed mess took on the appearance of something approaching barely edible. I opened the dishwasher, retrieved a clean plate and a fork, lifted the casserole dish over the plate, and raked out half the contents.

Bootsie glared at me reproachfully. "I'm sorry, girl," I commiserated as I put the casserole back on the burner, "but you'll just have to wait for it to cool."

The Irish setter looked skeptical, seemingly convinced this was merely an excuse on my part to deny her the banquet she so greatly deserved and to give it instead to some other dog in the neighborhood or perhaps even to the local homeless shelter down on the corner of Fifth and Main. I looked down at my plate, picked up the fork, and twirled a hefty portion of noodles around the tines, gently blowing against the rising steam. Then I gingerly tested the temperature against my tongue. Bootsie's eyes followed my every move.

The doorbell rang. "I'll get it," Lee called out.

Usually, Bootsie is the designated greeter for all visitors. Barking wildly, she normally beats both Lee and me to the front door, eager to meet the unwary. It takes a superhuman effort to restrain her enthusiasm, because not every person who shows up on our doorstep is ready for such a patented wet welcome.

But tonight Bootsie showed no interest in the unknown visitor. She had her one-track mind solidly anchored on the casserole cooling on the stove. I took one last bite of tuna, raked the uneaten portion back into the dish, and leaned over to set it on the floor. Impatient to get at its delectable contents, Bootsie almost knocked the dish from my hands.

"You stay here," I instructed the dog, "I'm going to see who's at the door." I could have just as easily been talking to the faucet, given the little attention she paid me. Well, there's one good thing that comes from this dog's singular preoccupation with food, I smiled to myself. At least I won't have to protect our visitor from seventy pounds of frenzied Irish setter.

On my way out of the kitchen, I grabbed a dish towel and wiped my hands, then dropped it haphazardly on the back of the sofa as I entered the living room. I still could not identify who stood on the threshold opposite Lee, since the solid wooden door completely hid the other person from my view.

As I walked up beside Lee, I heard her say, "I don't have time to play these silly games of yours—"

"What kind of silly games?" I interrupted.

Lee turned to me, an astonished expression on her face. "Then it's not you!" she exclaimed.

"Of course it's me," I answered. "What are you talking about?"

Lee, a perplexed look still gripping her face, pushed back against the door, opening it wider. For the first time, I was able to get a clear and unobstructed view of our visitor.

It was me.

CHAPTER 2

"After all,
what's a fairly normal housewife
to do
when she begins to suspect
she's married to a
monster?"

—Stokes Moran,

on Jessie Prichard Hunter's *Blood Music*

*O*r my spitting image, I should say.

As the man came into my view, and I suppose more importantly as I came into his, there was a moment when all three
of us—me, Lee, and the stranger—seemed suspended in
time. For the longest moment, none of us spoke. I looked at
him, he looked at me, Lee looked back and forth between the
two of us.

"What is this?" I finally asked.

He grinned. It was the strangest sensation watching his
face, *my* face, light up in a smile. I felt disconnected, disoriented, as if I were looking into an invisible mirror, but

beyond it, sort of like through an eternal looking glass. Little Alice certainly never felt more confused than I did at that instant.

"I'm your brother," he stated matter-of-factly. "I knew we were twins, but I never counted on us being identical twins."

I felt my equilibrium shatter, my solid inner core contract, my world shift. I was totally dumbfounded at his outrageous lie—I was an only child and knew beyond question that my parents had never had any other children. Yet the physical proof, which right now stared me stark in the face from not two feet away, seemed to substantiate his impossible claim. Again invoking the befuddled Alice, it was all getting curiouser and curiouser.

"I don't understand," I said.

"You and I were separated shortly after birth when we were both put up for adoption—"

"That's a lie."

"You mean you didn't know you were adopted?" he questioned, then looked shocked and dismayed at the sudden realization.

"It's not true." I shook my head. "It can't be true."

Lee, who had mutely observed this bizarre exchange, now spoke for the first time. "Why don't we move this family get-together inside?" she suggested, looking as stunned as I felt. "I think we'll all be more comfortable in the living room." The man nodded and walked past us into the house.

"What do you mean, 'family get-together'?" I whispered accusingly into her left ear as she closed the door behind him. "You're not buying this cock-and-bull story, are you?"

"Shoosh, he'll hear you." I was on the verge of telling her I didn't care whether he heard me or not, but she shook her head, then announced to our visitor, "Won't you please have a seat?"

"Just look at all these books," he said, gazing at the room's wall-to-wall, floor-to-ceiling shelves. "I don't think I've ever before seen this many books anywhere outside of the New York Public Library. You could open your own bookstore."

Lee laughed. "My husband is an avid mystery fan," she said, perching on the edge of the couch. "He's also a nationally syndicated mystery reviewer as well as a budding mystery novelist. In fact, a collection of his work is scheduled to be published this December."

"That's great," he said. "I had no idea I'd got me a famous brother."

"He writes under the name Stokes Moran. Maybe you've heard of it."

He shook his head. "No, can't say I have. But then I never cared much for mysteries. Except in real life, of course."

How droll, I thought.

Lee smiled up at him encouragingly. "Please, have a seat," she repeated, softly patting the cushion next to her. This time, he accepted the invitation. "Kyle." She nodded toward the recliner I normally occupied. But I stubbornly remained standing.

"I'm sure you can imagine our surprise, Mr. . . ." Lee waited for the automatic response. It came immediately.

"Oh, I'm sorry," he apologized. "In all the excitement, I plumb forgot to introduce myself. My name's Derek Winslow."

"And I'm Lee Malachi," my wife answered, then added with a frown, "and this is my somewhat recalcitrant husband, Kyle. But then, of course, you know that."

Derek nodded. "I've anticipated this moment for so long that I'm afraid my enthusiasm has unintentionally caused suspicion as well as confusion. Please forgive my thoughtlessness." He looked directly at me.

Despite my disbelief in his claim, as well as in his wordy apology, I had to admit that the physical resemblance between us was almost mirror perfect. Same height, same weight, same coloring, same facial features, even the same hairstyle. If there was any noticeable difference, I'd say his hair might have been just a tad longer than mine.

Lee laughed. "Well, to be honest with you, when I first saw you at the door, I thought you were my husband playing a practical joke on me."

I frowned. Lee was socializing with this stranger as if he were indeed a part of the family. I had no use for the Emily Post niceties and said as much.

"Lee, this is not the Mad Hatter's tea party," I said irritably, though Lord knows why I was currently wallowing in a Lewis Carroll rut. I glared suspiciously at Derek Winslow. "Just what is it you want?"

"Kyle!" Lee said, then turned to our guest. "Derek, you'll have to forgive my husband. I'm afraid all of this has been a bit of a shock for him."

Derek moved easily in his chair. "Oh, I understand." He smiled, and dammit, the bastard even had my teeth. "I'm not sure how I'd react either if someone suddenly appeared on my doorstep announcing that he was my long-lost brother. Especially if up to that moment I had never known I had a brother."

"Woof!" Bootsie, finally finished with her kitchen duty,

abruptly announced her presence. Derek blanched and tried to disappear into the sofa cushions as the dog approached.

"Heel, girl," I commanded. The sternness in my voice halted her in mid-stride, and I was able to intercept her before she had climbed all the way up into Derek's lap.

"She just wants to be friendly," I explained sullenly, dragging her by the collar toward the kitchen. "I'll just put her outside until we finish our business."

"I'm sorry to be so much trouble," I heard Derek telling Lee, "but me and dogs just don't get along." Then he couldn't be any brother of mine, I thought dismissively, as I shoved the Irish setter out into the backyard.

"Don't look at me like that," I said to the dumbfounded animal, who sat staring at me accusingly from the top step. "I don't know what's going on either."

I closed the door and walked back into the living room, where Derek and Lee now had drinks sitting in front of them on the coffee table.

"Kyle, would you like me to get you a club soda?" Lee asked.

"No, I would not." I looked directly at Derek. "I asked this question once before, but Bootsie intervened, so I'll ask it again. Just what is it you want?"

"I wish you'd loosen up a little," Derek said. "I know this is all somewhat overwhelming, but you're not making it very easy on me."

"And just why should I want to do that?"

Derek stood up. "I've dreamed of this moment for years, but I never envisioned it quite like this." He walked toward the front door.

Lee jumped from her seat and quickly followed him to the door. I ambled after them.

"Derek, wait," she pleaded. "Kyle's just being an ass," she said, frowning at me. "I'm sure if you'll just give him some time . . ."

Derek opened the door, turned, and smiled, looking directly at me. "I understand," he said. "I've had years to adjust to the news of my birth. I suppose I can't expect my brother to accept it in just a matter of minutes."

Lee reached for Derek's hand. "Will you call us later?"

"I tell you what," he said, accepting Lee's hand. "I'm staying at the Minuteman Inn out on Route 107. If Kyle wants to talk to me, he can see me there. I've got lots to say and, believe me, lots Kyle needs to hear. If he's interested, that is." He eyed me skeptically, then dropped Lee's hand from his grasp. "I'm in room 212, but I'll only be there till noon tomorrow."

Derek turned to leave, then paused and turned back, once again addressing me directly. "When I said I had dreamed about this moment, I was being quite literal. You see this knot on my thumb?" He held his right hand up for my inspection. "When I was a kid, I was told that it was the stub of a sixth finger that the doctor had cut off when I was born. But a few years ago I dreamed that it was really a physical link with my twin, a connection that was severed at birth.

"You may not believe this," he added, smiling wistfully, "but I had that dream a long time before I ever knew about your existence."

He looked at me expectantly. I said nothing. Derek waited for another minute. Did I detect a look of sadness in his eyes?

Or was it anger? Finally he said good-bye to Lee, and she closed the door behind him.

"I'm ashamed of you," my wife said. "I've never seen you behave so badly. You were downright rude. Kyle, he's quite possibly your brother, and you weren't even polite to him."

I nodded, not really listening, wondering what in the world was going on, all the time rubbing the virtually invisible but suddenly throbbing bump on my left thumb.

CHAPTER 3

"The solution
is not so much shocking
as it is cautionary—
that sometimes
maybe we'd be better off
if we'd just practice a little
kindness."

—Stokes Moran,

on Charlene Weir's *Consider the Crows*

"*He*'s lying," I said.

More than an hour had passed since Derek's departure. After her initial outburst, Lee had somewhat moderated her opinion on my uncharacteristic behavior and had, for the last few minutes, been attempting to persuade me to view Derek's assertions with a more open mind.

"I believe him," she said.

"Why?"

"For one thing, he has the physical evidence on his side. You can't deny he looks exactly like you."

"Everybody supposedly has a double," I argued. "Maybe Derek just happens to be mine."

"Yeah, sure. And next I suppose you'll claim it's a result of plastic surgery."

"Well, it could be," I said.

Lee slammed her hand down on the sofa's armrest. "Why? What reason could Derek possibly have to be anything other than what he says he is—your brother?"

"I don't know what his reason might be," I said, rubbing my left thumb for perhaps the hundredth time in the last sixty minutes. "It's just too preposterous to be believed."

Lee stood up. "You're the one who's being too preposterous to be believed. I'm going to make a pot of coffee."

I followed my wife into the kitchen and watched her empty the stale remains of this morning's brew, wash out the carafe, fill it with fresh water, and pour the liquid into the top of the automatic coffeemaker. She then snapped open the side of the appliance, removed the soggy container of old grounds, retrieved a pristine filter from the pack that sits conveniently next to the coffeemaker, positioned the filter into its proper place, and dumped two tablespoons of coffee onto the white paper. I observed my wife performing this totally routine and unremarkable domestic task with an inexplicable sense of detachment and isolation.

Lee looked at me. "Did you want any?" I nodded, and she turned back to her ministrations, adding more water and another heaping tablespoonful of coffee to the mix. She then placed the carafe on the burner and programmed the digital control to "Brew."

"You've never talked very much about your parents," she commented, still facing away from me, her voice low. "About the only thing I know is that they've both been dead for twenty years."

What could I tell her about my parents? That I never really knew them? That, as an only child, I had to create my own little world, separate and apart from theirs? That, whenever I was in their presence, I had always felt like an outsider, an interloper? What? What could I tell my wife about two people who had basically remained strangers to me my entire life?

Bootsie interrupted whatever response I might have given. She scratched against the back door, reminding me that I had never retrieved her from her backyard exile following Derek's abrupt departure. I walked over to the door and let her in.

Prancing excitedly, the dog entered the kitchen demanding her usual treat for good behavior—a Milk-Bone dog biscuit. As I fished one out of the box and placed it between Bootsie's jaws, Lee lifted two coffee cups off the mug tree and forcefully plunked them down on the breakfast bar.

The moment for me to answer Lee's question had passed. My wife's body language communicated her hurt feelings, but she said nothing. The silence between us grew uncomfortable, her question left pending, hanging like a cold heavy fog.

I knew Lee was taking my nonresponsiveness as a personal rebuff. But, at this moment, I didn't know how to answer her, not even how to bridge the immense gulf that had suddenly yawned beneath our feet.

This was the first time in our short married life that Lee and I had been reminded how little we really knew each other. I realized that we would indeed face all sorts of personal land mines in our future life together. But why did we have to stumble into one just now? Damn Derek and his preposterous lie!

But was it really a lie? Didn't it now all make sense? Didn't this explain the sense of separation I'd always felt toward my parents? Wasn't I just being stubborn in rejecting Derek's claim? Could it be possible that I really did have a brother?

These are the thoughts I should have been sharing with Lee, discussing the problem openly and logically with my wife. But there was some failing inside me, some basic inadequacy I recognized but could not define, some emotional Red Sea that adamantly refused to part. I caught myself rubbing the nub on my thumb again.

"The coffee's ready," Lee announced without inflection, cradling her mug in both hands and gingerly sipping its contents.

I reached for the other mug, now sitting alone on the counter, filled it with the steaming liquid, then leaned back against the bar. "Lee," I began.

"Not now, Kyle." She gazed into the coffee's black depths, and I glimpsed a single tear ease from the corner of her eye and start a haphazard trail down her right cheek.

"Lee," I repeated.

A knock came. The back door opened, and my next-door neighbor, Nolan James, stuck his head around the frame.

"Anybody home?" he asked redundantly, stepping into the kitchen, Bootsie rising to greet him.

"Excuse me," Lee muttered, scampering from the room.

"I don't think your wife likes me," Nolan remarked while bending down and scratching Bootsie between the ears.

"It's not you, Nolan," I said. "It's something else entirely."

"I wouldn't be so sure. Remember, I tried to tell you that I didn't think she had ever really forgiven me for taking those safety-deposit box keys."*

I laughed. "Trust me, Nolan. That's not it."

"Then why does she always find some excuse to avoid me every time we meet up. Answer me that."

"That's not true."

"Of course it is." Nolan patted Bootsie on the rear, then joined me at the bar. "You just watch her the next time I get near. See how she reacts."

I decided to concede the point. "Nolan, would you like some coffee?"

"Sure thing," he answered, lifting an empty mug off the ceramic tree. "You look worried about something. Is it the missus?" he added with a grin.

I filled him in on the whole bizarre episode with Derek. Nolan, in addition to being a talkative know-it-all as well as a helpful friend, is also a retired police detective, and I've often found his observations and his advice to be especially useful.

"What are you going to do?" he asked when I had finished relating the evening's events.

"What do you mean, what am I going to do?"

"Surely you're not just going to sit around and do nothing, are you?"

"What do you suggest I do?"

"Check him out. See if his story holds up. Run him through the FBI files."

"And just how would I go about doing that?"

Nolan grinned. "Well, I might be able to help you out there."

*See *And Then There Were Ten* (Scribner, 1995).

"I thought you were retired."

He laughed. "I still have my little ways of getting things done," he said mysteriously.

I shrugged. "Then go for it."

Nolan pulled a pocket-sized notebook out of his pants. A three-inch pencil stuck out of the spiral top. He knocked the pad against the edge of the counter, and the pencil popped out.

"I guess you always come prepared," I commented.

"Just like a Boy Scout," he said. "A little habit I picked up after twenty years on the force. Now, tell me all you know about this man."

"Well," I started, "he's—"

Nolan cut me off. "Name first."

"Derek Winslow."

"Address?"

"I don't know."

"Home phone number?"

"I don't know."

"Occupation?"

"I don't know."

Nolan dropped the pad and pencil down on the top of the bar. "You don't know anything, do you?"

"I know his name. And that he claims to be my brother—"

"Your identical twin brother," Nolan interrupted.

"Yeah," I admitted. "So that gives you the physical description right there. He looks just like me. Write that down."

"And I guess you'd both be the same age too?"

"Makes sense to me," I admitted sarcastically.

"Which is?"

"Which is what?" I was enjoying Nolan's comic cat-and-mouse routine.

"Your age."

"Oh, that," I said. "Forty-one."

Nolan closed the notebook. "I suppose I've got enough, then, to run a routine check." He stood up and walked toward the back door. "I'll let you know if anything turns up on this weirdo."

I couldn't resist what I knew was an intentional trap. "What makes you call him a weirdo?"

"Well, you have to admit," he drawled, "anybody wanting you as a brother has got to be just a little bit off in the head." Nolan darted behind the door.

I laughed. "Oh yeah?" I looked around for something to throw, spotted Bootsie's box of Milk-Bones that I had left sitting out on the counter, picked up the whole box, and threw it at Nolan's retreating figure. The box crashed against the closing door and spilled its contents all over the floor.

Bootsie lunged for the treats. I left her happily munching on the unexpected doggie bonanza and turned my attention toward the immediate problem of mending fences with my wife. I found Lee upstairs, already bedded down, her head obscured by a copy of *Family Circle*. I intentionally bumped against the edge of the water bed so she'd know I was in the room, but the magazine never once wavered. She continued to hide behind its pages.

I undressed, then performed my nightly bathroom rituals, and eventually returned to the bedroom. Lee still stubbornly persisted with the periodical. It seemed obvious that she was waiting for me to break the silence.

"I never loved my parents," I suddenly blurted. No, that wasn't right. I had loved them, in a fashion, as best I knew how to love at the time, I suppose. It was more that I never understood why I had always found it so difficult to express my feelings for my parents, so hard just to say those three simple little words "I love you." So hard, in fact, that at some point I surmised maybe the love hadn't ever been there. No time now to explain all those complexities to my wife, so I just let my bald statement stand.

Lee's face slowly came into view as the magazine finally lowered.

"I always thought it was some failing in me," I said. "Like I was a bad son. It never occurred to me that maybe the problem wasn't with me at all."

Lee reached down and flipped back the covers, invitingly patting the space beside her. I climbed onto the bed, barely conscious of the resulting wave. I leaned over and kissed her.

"So you're starting to believe Derek's story?" Lee asked after we broke from our embrace.

"I'm not sure," I said, resting my head against her shoulder. "But I'm certainly more willing to listen to what he has to say."

"Then you've decided to talk with him again before he leaves?"

I nodded. "I don't see how I can let him get away without at least hearing him out," I said, once again rubbing the nub on my left thumb. "Who knows? I might get a brother out of the deal."

"I'm glad," Lee said, planting a kiss on the top of my head.

"That's more like the Kyle I know." She stretched over and switched off the light.

I shifted toward her, hands and mouth seeking out familiar spots.

"That's more like the Kyle I know too," she murmured contentedly.

CHAPTER 4

*"The hero
must come to terms
not so much with his own
mortality
as with the mortality
of those people
who are closest to him."*

—Stokes Moran,

on Lawrence Block's *The Devil Knows You're Dead*

"There's still no answer." I replaced the telephone receiver back on its plastic cradle for the third time within the last two hours.

"Maybe he's at breakfast," Lee suggested.

I frowned. "That's what I thought when I called at eight o'clock," I said. "It even remained a possibility at nine. But I can't imagine anyone lingering more than a couple of hours over their bacon and eggs."

Lee smiled. "It seems to me that there have been occasions when you and I have enjoyed some rather leisurely breakfasts."

"That's right," I agreed, "but, if I remember correctly, those breakfasts had nothing to do with food."

"Well"—Lee winked—"maybe Derek also has other items on his breakfast menu."

I shook my head. "I don't think so," I said. "If I read him right, his number one priority right now is getting together with his supposedly long-lost brother. This morning I can't see him doing anything else except sitting expectantly by the phone."

"Then where is he?" Lee asked.

I shrugged. "That's what I'd like to know."

Lee and I stood across the kitchen bar from each other. I had slept fitfully the night before, alternating between unfocused dreams of my spartan childhood and surrealistic images of obscene circus freaks joined grotesquely at the thumbs. I had awakened at 6 A.M., body weary and brain tired.

"Would you like some more coffee?" Lee asked.

I shook my head. "Four cups is two more than my usual quota."

In between my phone calls to Derek's motel room, I had managed to slip into my jogging clothes, take Bootsie for her morning run along the Yessula River, munch down a couple of pieces of toast, and intake more caffeine than my personal ecosystem could logically absorb. For the first time in several months, I craved a cigarette. Best not to admit that weakness to my wife, however.

"Maybe he left already," Lee said.

Again I shook my head. "No," I answered. "Derek gave me until noon, and he would stay right up until the last minute."

"How do you know that?" Lee argued. "After the way you acted toward him yesterday, he might have just decided the hell with you."

"Uh-uh." I felt adamant. "I can't see him giving up on this no matter how hurt or angry he may have felt."

"How can you be so sure?"

"Because I wouldn't," I said.

Lee reached across the countertop and caressed my hand. "You've finally accepted the fact that he's your brother, haven't you, Kyle?"

I nodded.

"What changed your mind?"

"Oh, I don't know." I hesitated, then added, "Several things, I suppose." Then I told her about the bump on my left thumb.

"Why didn't you mention that earlier?" Lee seemed incredulous. "How could you not immediately believe Derek when he told you about the same thing on his thumb?"

"I don't know," I repeated. "Shock, denial, confusion. Hell, I don't know." My head ached. "It didn't seem quite so con-clusive yesterday."

Lee frowned. "That's impossible."

"I'm not good with feelings," I admitted. "I never have been. I guess I just needed time to sort everything out."

"And while you sort, your brother walks out of your life for-ever. Kyle, how could you!"

"I keep telling you," I enunciated carefully. "Derek hasn't gone anywhere."

"Then prove it."

"How?" I demanded.

"Stop fooling around with the damn phone and go find out for yourself."

"All right, I will."

"Good," she yelled.

"Good," I yelled back.

"Action has to follow words," Lee goaded.

Furiously, I grabbed the keys to the Land Rover off the peg next to the back door, stormed out to the driveway, almost stripped the car's gears backing it out onto the street, and was halfway down the block when I realized I had walked out of the house still wearing my jogging togs. What's worse, since this outfit had no pockets, I also realized that my wallet, which contained my money, ID, and especially my driver's license, still sat orphaned on the nightstand next to my bed. The hell with it, I decided. Just let a cop try to stop me. I was on my way to see my brother.

Finally.

Tipton, Connecticut, is just three whistle-stops this side of the New York state line. More than half of the town's nine thousand white-collar inhabitants commute into Manhattan or its metropolitan environs on a daily basis. Most of the nine-to-fivers are forced to catch the 7:22 A.M. Metro-North into Grand Central, but some of the luckier ones—those not quite so rushed, due either to the status of their jobs or to their lack thereof—are able to grab a later train. Thus it was some of those favored few that I spied milling around outside the depot as I crossed the tracks and pulled out onto Route 107, known locally as Jasmine Boulevard.

I glanced at my watch. The train the commuters were waiting for would be the 10:10 from Riverton. Somehow that timetable didn't have quite the murderous ring to it as, say, the 4:50 from Paddington in Agatha Christie's famous mystery story American readers know more familiarly as *What Mrs. McGillicuddy Saw!* And it certainly didn't come close to the romance and intrigue of *Murder on the Orient Express*, another Christie classic that inexplicably became Americanized as *Murder on the Calais Coach*.

Strange, I thought, that a writer with the sales and stature of Agatha Christie would allow such unwarranted American effrontery. Surely her books could have retained their original titles had she insisted. And it wasn't just a once-in-a-while happenstance. Christie endured innumerable title changes during her long career. *Dumb Witness* became the even dumber *Poirot Loses a Client, Five Little Pigs* got stuck with *Murder in Retrospect,* and *Sparkling Cyanide* dissolved into *Remembered Death.*

Perhaps the only justifiable tinkering with Christie's titles came with the 1940 Dodd, Mead publication of *And Then There Were None,* a brilliant substitute for the overtly racist *Ten Little Niggers.* With so many liberties so freely taken, it's a wonder *The Murder of Roger Ackroyd, The ABC Murders,* and *The Pale Horse* made their American debuts unaltered. Thankfully, *Curtain* escaped the indignity of being rehung as *Drapes.*

I suddenly found myself steering the car into the parking lot of the Minuteman Inn, with absolutely no recollection of making the requisite twists and turns necessary to have arrived at this point. Heading toward an unpredictable but almost certainly emotional encounter, I had followed precedent and lapsed into the safe and comfortable environment of mystery novels. I rebuked myself that Agatha Christie, no matter how pleasant a medicine, was not a panacea for real life.

I pulled the Land Rover into one of the vacant parking slots near the Inn's front entrance. The Minuteman is the only motel in the whole of Tipton, but since the town really doesn't have any tourist attractions, the motel serves more as a meeting place for the community than a stopover for travelers. Each week, the Inn's banquet room plays host to our local civic organizations. On Monday noon, it's the Rotarians, on Tuesday the Lions, on Wednesday the Junior League, and on Friday the Chamber of Commerce. Thursday remains open in case the Boy Scouts or the Young Republicans require an emergency conference. No one in Tipton meets on weekends; Saturdays and Sundays are strictly reserved for golf, tennis, and brunch at the local country club. While I have never personally participated in any of these activities, as a good citizen of Tipton I am nonetheless privy to their schedules, thanks to the *Journal Express*, the weekly town newspaper, which continues to recycle these tired functions as if they are cosmic events.

Glancing once again at my watch and verifying the time was nowhere near noon, I entered the Minuteman's lobby, walked past the entrance to the dining room, loped up the stairs two at a time, and emerged onto the second floor. Room 212 turned out to be just three doors down from the stairwell. A maid's cart sat unattended right in the middle of the hallway.

I squeezed between the cart and the wall and knocked on the door.

I waited. No response.

I knocked again.

"Derek," I called out. "Derek, it's Kyle."

Still nothing.

I knocked louder. I yelled. I pounded. Not a sound came from inside the room.

Incited, I suppose, by the commotion, the motel maid stuck her head out of the adjacent room.

"Cut the noise, fella," she complained with a frown. "I got a headache that won't quit."

"Take an Excedrin," I said, then returned to beating down the door.

"Easy, guy," she said, emerging into the hallway. Her bulk forced me to back up against the cart.

The maid was large-boned and tall, but not exactly what I would call fat, and she had a florid complexion that was topped by gray-streaked red hair. "Now, what's all the excitement?" she asked.

"This is my brother's room," I said, trying to keep the anxiety out of my voice, "and I can't get him to answer."

"Are you sure he hasn't checked out?"

Again, I had overlooked an obvious explanation. I silently kicked myself for not asking after Derek at the front desk. But no—as soon as I considered the possibility that Derek might have checked out, I rejected it. He simply would not just up and leave, not until he had given me every opportunity to relent.

I shook my head. "He's expecting me."

The maid's right hand magically produced a ring of keys from a hidden fold in her uniform. "I was just about to clean in here," she said, inserting the correct key into the lock. "But you stay here," she warned, eyeing me sternly.

"Yes, ma'am," I replied meekly.

She opened the door. "Anyone in here?" she called as she entered. Ignoring the potential consequences, I followed silently in her wake.

The room was dark. No lights were on, and the drawn curtains effectively blocked the outside sunshine. Even in the dimness, I could see that the bed was unmade, the clothes Derek had worn the previous night were draped neatly over the back of a chair, and his open suitcase lay flat and unpacked on the top of the dresser. Against the beige carpet, I spied one black loafer peeking timidly out from the edge of the bed's trailing coverlet.

This was definitely Derek's room. The only thing missing was Derek himself.

The maid looked at me, frowning her disapproval that I had not remained in the hallway as promised. Without vocally admonishing me, she moved quietly toward the open bathroom door.

It wasn't like in the movies. The maid didn't suddenly let go with an ear-piercing scream. All I heard was an audible intake of breath. I eased around her rigid stance and peered through the doorway.

Derek lay naked on the bathroom floor, his body curled in a fetal position, his head resting easily against the cold tiles. He simply looked asleep, but it didn't take Kay Scarpetta to tell me he was dead.

CHAPTER 5

*"The author
creates characters
who refuse to behave
in acceptable fashion,
who become so real
in the reader's imagination
that they linger
long after the party's over,
like guests who don't know
when to go home."*

—Stokes Moran,

on Sue Grafton's *"D" Is for Deadbeat*

"Go home, Nolan," I muttered irritably.

"Go home?" he responded incredulously. "You're the one who asked me to come down here in the first place, remember?"

I remembered.

After making our startling discovery, the maid—whose name I then learned was Peggy O'Malley—went to inform the motel's management while I called the police. Not wanting to disturb any possible evidence in Derek's room, Peggy had considerately offered me the use of the telephone in room 210, the unoccupied unit she had just finished cleaning next door to 212. I dutifully reported Derek's death to Tipton's

45

finest, and then, in quick succession, I also dialed up both Lee and Nolan. My wife, while understandably shocked and dismayed, agreed to wait at home for my return. Nolan, on the other hand, beat the cops to the scene.

As an ex–homicide detective, Nolan has proved quite effective in dealing with the authorities when, from time to time, I have found myself in potentially difficult or embarrassing situations. And today had been no exception.

When the uniforms finally arrived on the scene, Nolan quickly explained in a sort of shorthand cop-speak exactly those events that had eventually led to the discovery of Derek's body, sparing me the uncomfortable moment of defending why I had rebuffed my twin brother the night before. He accomplished all this without exposing any of the personal details with which I still had not come to terms.

But that had been half an hour ago. In the interim, the police—the first unit had since been joined by two plain-clothesmen as well as by a local physician whose Tipton office serves as a semi-satellite operation for the Greenwich medical examiner—had been fully occupied in their official duties, and Nolan and I had been banished to room 210 for the duration. You have no idea how long thirty minutes can be when Nolan, like an old firehorse back under the familiar harness, gushes forth with a nonstop verbal Vesuvius of past glories. After hearing for the third time his glorious exploits in the McAllister case, I finally lost my patience.

"I said go home," I repeated.

"Are you serious?" His voice sounded aggrieved. I suddenly realized that perhaps my irritation had really been self-directed and that Nolan had only been a convenient target. I apologized.

"Nolan, I'm sorry," I said. "I'm still having trouble accepting Derek's death."

"I understand," he responded, patting me gently on the arm.

Nolan and I both sat perched on the edge of Peggy's freshly made-up bed, sunlight pouring through the open curtains, dust motes visible in the air, traffic noises filtering up from the street, men bumping around in the room next door. Great, I thought, just what I needed—Nolan understands.

But I knew I sure as hell didn't.

I was emotionally blocked. My mind was all clogged up, filled to distension with unresolved, undisgorged contradictions. How did I feel about Derek? A man who less than twenty-four hours ago I hadn't even known existed, a man whom I had seen for only a brief few minutes, a man who for all intents and purposes still remained a total stranger to me. Yet finally, and, yes, grudgingly, I had accepted him as my brother. Not that he would ever know of my acknowledgment. I had arrived too late at the recognition for it to hold any meaning for him, and he was now damn sure beyond caring.

I saw once again that indelible image—Derek naked against the white bathroom tiles. But it wasn't Derek I was seeing—it was me. It was my body lying there, my body that was now being probed and prodded in the next room by unknown hands, my body that death had unceremoniously visited. But that couldn't be. I was alive; it was Derek who was dead. But that wasn't right either. We had come from the same source, we had shared the same human space for nine months. If I was alive, Derek should have been alive too. It didn't make sense any other way. But, since Derek was dead, then that meant I must be living on borrowed time. Twins, identical, one and the same. I shook my head. No, I concluded, God had simply made a terrible mistake. Or, as a horrendous alternative suddenly emerged fully formed in my thoughts, perhaps it had not been God at all.

A peremptory knock interrupted my muddled thoughts. The door opened, and two men entered the motel room.

Nolan stood up, shook hands, and greeted the two like old friends. I belatedly got to my feet, and Nolan performed the introductions.

The taller of the two Nolan identified as Sergeant Pitkin. The other I recognized, from pictures I'd seen in the *Tipton Journal Express*, as Dr. Nathan Harris, a local MD who also served the town as an auxiliary coroner. The medical examiner's office, located some six miles away in Greenwich, did not normally respond to apparently routine calls.

"I understand the deceased was your brother," Pitkin said after we had shaken hands. His eyes narrowed. "I can definitely see the resemblance," he added.

I nodded.

Seemingly satisfied with my nonverbal response, Pitkin continued. "We've finished up in there"—he gestured toward the adjoining room—"and you're free to go. I appreciate your staying around, but I don't think we'll need anything beyond what Nolan here has already told us." He paused, cleared his throat, then proceeded. "There doesn't appear to be any evidence of foul play, and the doc here says it without a doubt looks like a heart attack." Pitkin looked for confirmation to Dr. Harris, who just marginally tilted his head in agreement.

"In cases like this," Pitkin continued, seemingly having been elected speaker by default, "where there appears to be no dispute as to the cause of death, we usually go ahead and release the body for burial." He paused, then added, "Do you have a local mortician? If not, I'll be happy to recommend one."

I wondered if he got a kickback for the referral, then I dismissed the notion as an overdose of crime-fiction cynicism.

"I want an autopsy," I said.

"I-I r-really d-don't s-s-see the n-n-n-need," Dr. Harris stuttered nervously. Was this a normal speech problem, or had I somehow upset him?

"An autopsy would take at the earliest a couple of days," Sergeant Pitkin interrupted, "perhaps as much as a week, and we'd have to send the body all the way over to Greenwich. I'm sure you don't want to put the family through such a delay."

His unctuousness irritated me. "As far as I know, the only family Derek has is me, and I don't mind in the least waiting for the results," I said smilingly.

"Very well," Pitkin said. "We'll be in touch." He turned to leave.

"B-but the b-b-budget," Dr. Harris wailed at Pitkin's heels.

The door closed behind them.

"Not two of nature's noblest specimens, I'll grant you," Nolan commented after they had gone. "But just why are you insisting on an autopsy? As much as I hate to say it, I agree with Pitkin. I didn't see anything particularly suspicious about the death."

I shook my head. "You didn't see Derek last night." How could I explain my feelings to Nolan when I couldn't even clarify them for myself. I felt my left thumb twinge. "He was as healthy as me," I amplified, "and you don't see me falling over dead."

"Kyle, that's not rational. For all you know, Derek could have had a serious heart condition. Remember, while you may have been brothers, this man was still a stranger to you."

I shrugged, ignoring the common sense of his argument. "It's my right to request an autopsy, isn't it?"

"Yes." Nolan tried to suppress a smile, but his eyes gave him away.

"And if this were New York, it wouldn't even be an issue, would it?"

"That's true," Nolan admitted, folding his arms across his chest. "Autopsies are automatic in New York State."

I opened the door, suddenly eager to leave.

"But what's your point?" Nolan persisted. "After all, this is Connecticut, not New York."

"Just say I'm doing my bit for better government," I commented, and walked out the door.

With Lee in Manhattan performing her agenting duties, I spent the next two days back in book review harness, reading the Grafton as well as two other mystery novels, writing the reviews, and faxing them off to the syndication service. If Derek's autopsy showed anything interesting, I didn't want my professional commitments to interfere with the plan that was slowly taking shape in my mind. With three reviews in the can, I would be able to buy myself a little breathing space, if the need arose. And I was certain it would.

Since the police were convinced Derek had died from natural causes, they had neither attempted to collect any evidence from his motel room nor bothered to cordon it off. No POLICE LINE—DO NOT CROSS banner blocked entry to room 212.

So, with Nolan in tow and before leaving the Minuteman Inn the morning of Derek's death, I had paid a week's rent on 212 and had instructed the manager to keep the maid as well as the morbidly curious totally away from the room. I didn't want any potential evidence being disturbed, though I certainly didn't share my ulterior motive with the manager.

But I did share it with my wife, which turned out to be a big mistake. Lee, when I told her of what I had done, thought I was crazy. Before her departure for New York, she had even said as much.

"You're crazy," she had said.

Nolan just shook his head over my antics and tut-tutted something about how I was "living in a fantasy world." Bootsie was the only one who didn't question my sanity, and I knew her conditional support would last only so long as I remained the one who daily dished out her Purina Dog Chow. Mess with her food, and Bootsie's loyalty would quickly be up for sale.

But I had to admit, in those moments of quiet reflection when I was able to coolly assess the situation, I too could not defend the logic of my action. All I had was an instinct, a gut feeling, that something was wrong.

For one thing, Derek had finally reached the end of his search. Only tragic irony would have allowed him to die before he could be united with his long-lost brother. And I didn't believe in tragic irony. Cruel fate, yes—tragic irony, no.

But perhaps the overriding reason for my disbelief in natural causes was that I didn't want to face my own mortality. Accident, suicide, or murder—any one of the three would have been preferable to learning that my genes were flawed, that something within my body was suspect, that whatever had killed Derek might also kill me. I didn't want to accept that pronouncement, so I eagerly embraced any other conceivable alternatives. But the alternatives weren't all that appealing either.

Accident? I have never heard of an accidental heart attack, so that possibility had to be nonexistent.

Suicide? Disregarding the implausibility of a self-induced heart attack, had Derek wanted to kill himself, I was totally convinced he would not have picked that particular moment. He had too much interest in completing the little drama he had started the night before to leave prior to the final curtain. If he had harbored the slightest hope that I would knock on his door—and I believed he did—he would have waited to the last second, and then some. No. Suicide was not an option.

And that left murder. It remained a clear choice between those two—either Derek had died from natural causes, as everyone but me insisted, or else somebody had killed him. And that's the horrendous conclusion I had reached standing in room 210 the morning of Derek's death. With absolutely no proof, and surely lacking any certifiably sane reasoning, I had nevertheless deduced my own brother's murder. Holmes and Poirot would have drummed me out of the detective corps, and Spade and Marlowe would have laughed me out of town. I didn't care that I was a failure at deductive reasoning, I just knew how I felt. And now I was waiting, hoping for something—anything—that would back me up.

CHAPTER 6

*"Murder is
indeed the great equalizer,
bringing
everything else
down to its scurrilous level."*

—Stokes Moran,

on P. D. James's *A Taste for Death*

"You mean Derek was murdered!"

Under any other circumstances, Lee's stunned over-the-phone incredulity would have been enormously satisfying, with a smirking "I told you so" lingering unspoken between us, gold mine ammunition for future use.

But these were not normal circumstances, and I could generate no joy at being proved right. My brother—a man who remained as much a mystery to me as on the night he had first appeared on my doorstep—had been murdered. The autopsy had confirmed my unsubstantiated hunch.

"Yes," I answered my wife, content with that simple nonaccusatory reply.

"I've been trying to reach you for hours," she said testily. "Is that all you've got to say?"

All for the moment, I could have answered. But I was too exhausted to form the words. Instead, I collapsed in the welcome comfort of the La-Z-Boy recliner. It had been a long afternoon.

Seven days had elapsed since Derek's death before I finally heard back from Pitkin. When he telephoned, he had been terse, asking only that I meet him immediately at the Minuteman Inn. I didn't have to ask which room.

When I got there, the door stood open. Within the confines of the small room, Pitkin and two uniformed officers were busily occupied with basic police work. One man was dusting for fingerprints, another was putting some of Derek's personal belongings in what looked like a plastic garbage bag. Pitkin himself was down on all fours inspecting the carpet. After a minute, he looked up, saw me standing in the doorway, and beckoned me inside.

"It was murder," Pitkin said, rising to his feet. "The coroner says Winslow died of digitoxin poisoning. What we're doing now is collecting evidence to see if we can determine by what agent the poison was administered."

The good sergeant offered no apology, showed no remorse, and gave no acknowledgment that had it not been for me there would have been no evidence to gather. Instead, he bulled ahead with the question he should have asked a week earlier.

"Do you have any idea who might have killed your brother?"

"I'm sure you remember what Nolan told you that first day," I reminded him. "Until Derek showed up on my doorstep the evening before, I didn't even know he existed."

"What does that—" he began, but I cut him off.

"So how could I possibly know who might have wanted him dead?"

"But didn't he say anything—"

Again, I interrupted his question. "I didn't give Derek much of a chance to say anything. His sudden appearance in my life, claiming not only that he was my brother but that I had been adopted—"

This time he interrupted me. "You mean to say you never knew about that either?"

I smiled. "That's right, Sergeant. So you see, Derek Winslow is as much a stranger to me as he is to you. I'm also afraid that I know no more than you do about his murder."

Pitkin frowned. "Then why did you demand an autopsy? From all indications, there was absolutely no reason to believe his death was anything but a heart attack."

I rubbed my thumb. "Just call it the tie that binds."

"That doesn't make any sense," he claimed.

"Neither would anything I said." I walked over to the dressing table and looked in the mirror—at my face, at Derek's face. Again, how could I get Pitkin to understand a paradox without explanation. It was best not even to try.

Through the mirror, I saw Pitkin reach inside his coat pocket and retrieve a small spiral-bound notebook.

"Can I get your address, Mr. Malachi?"

"What for?" I demanded. I turned to face him.

"I need it for our records. I failed to get it the last time we met, so when I called you, I had to look your number up in the telephone book."

Too much effort for you, huh? In case you failed to notice it, you half-brain, my address is also listed in the directory, I thought perhaps a mite too unkindly. But, like the respectful and law-abiding citizen that I am, I complied with his request anyway.

"Does this mean you're finished with me?" I asked, after he had written down my street address and closed the notebook.

Pitkin nodded. "I'll be contacting you again if anything turns up."

"I take it I'm not a suspect."

For the first time, he not only cracked a smile, he actually laughed. "Not likely. If you were the killer, you had a perfect murder on your hands. I can't see you spoiling that."

"A perfect murder." I paused for a moment. "I trust that won't be the case."

"What do you mean?"

"Sergeant Pitkin, if it's a perfect murder, then we'll never catch the killer."

"I didn't mean it like that," he said. "Believe me, sooner or later we'll get our man."

"I certainly hope so." I turned to leave.

"Oh, one last thing," Pitkin added.

"Yes?" With a sigh, I faced him once again.

"The body's ready to be released. Did you ever contact a mortuary?"

The cold, anonymous manner in which he referred to Derek angered me, but I kept my temper in check. After all, I needed a favor.

"Could you get the coroner to hold Derek's body for a little while longer?" I asked.

"Whatever for?"

"I need a little time."

Pitkin frowned. "Time for what? Look, we don't have room to keep dead bodies just hanging around."

Pitkin was such an ass he had absolutely no inkling how his inadvertent imagery had shuddered my spine. I decided to give him a jolt as well.

"Because," I responded coldly, "I need a few days to track down Derek's killer."

"You should have seen the look on Pitkin's face." Lee, Nolan, and I stood bunched around the breakfast bar the next morning, coffee mugs cradled in our hands.

Nolan and I laughed. Lee, only minutes back from her latest New York sojourn and fully informed for the first time of my recent activities, did not quite share the joke.

"Kyle, you can't be serious," she objected. "This is a matter for the police."

I drained the good-to-the-last-drop liquid and gingerly placed my empty coffee mug on the counter. But before I could outline the plan I had been formulating for the last few days, Nolan interrupted.

"You'd have to know Pitkin to appreciate the situation," Nolan said. "I'm sure Kyle was just tweaking that stupid cop's big fat nose."

I had never before heard Nolan criticize a member of his former profession. If Will Rogers had never met a man he didn't like, then Nolan James had never met a policeman he didn't respect. Until now, that is.

"Pitkin's a real pain in the ass," Nolan continued. "Even the guys down at the station don't have any use for him."

"Now you tell me," I said. "Why didn't you say something earlier?"

Nolan looked sheepish. "I guess I just didn't see the purpose."

"I don't understand," I said.

Nolan poured himself a second cup of coffee. Standing with his back turned to us, he muttered, "I thought Pitkin was right."

"You didn't believe Derek was murdered?" I demanded, feeling momentarily betrayed, then realizing as I did so that the professional detective in the man would never have allowed him to jump to such an unsupported conclusion.

Nolan turned around, grinning. "To tell you the truth, I thought you were a nut. There wasn't a shred of evidence to suggest anything but natural causes."

I was confused. "But you backed me up on my autopsy request?"

He nodded. "It was your right to ask for one. It didn't matter that I thought you were off your rocker." To take the sting out of his words, Nolan slapped me on the back, then propped his elbows on the counter, and looked up at me with hound dog eyes. Lee and I both burst out laughing.

"Darling," Lee commented after a minute of silence, "what did start you thinking it was murder? You never told me."

Here was the critical moment. How could I explain my thought processes without sounding like a total idiot? Oh, what the hell, I thought.

"I wanted it to be murder," I said finally, sounding like the very fool I hadn't wanted to admit I was. No self-respecting mystery writer would ever have allowed a fictional character to get away with something this preposterous. But here I was—lifelong mystery reader, professional mystery reviewer, gestating mystery writer—confessing to just such an absurdity. I'm sure not even Miss Marple had ever observed such an aberration of human behavior.

"You wanted it to be murder?" Lee echoed my statement in total wonderment.

I nodded. Tongue-tied, I tried to match words to my feelings. "I don't expect you to understand," I began, "but when I saw Derek lying there dead on that floor, I had"—I searched for the most appropriate description—"I guess you'd call it an out-of-body experience."

I paused, expecting some sort of derisive protest from either Lee or Nolan. Encountering only quizzical facial expressions, I continued.

"It was somehow me—my body—not Derek's. And I knew something was wrong. I knew it simply wasn't my time to go."

I paused again. Still, neither Lee nor Nolan spoke. I interpreted their silence as a positive force, willing me to unlock their understanding, encouraging me to persuade them of my illogical logic.

"And I also knew that I wouldn't have killed myself either. Not after finding my brother, not after all these years." I stopped, shrugged, started to enunciate a further defense, then abandoned the unspoken attempt.

Lee finally supplied the necessary conclusion. "So it had to be murder," she said, putting an end to my self-imposed discomfort.

I nodded. Whether she actually believed my fantastic explanation, I felt she had nevertheless accepted the conviction of my feelings. I knew she had to be skeptical—what sane person wouldn't be?—but she was also showing blind faith in her eccentric husband. And I loved her for that. Smiling, I leaned over and planted a kiss on her lips. In turn, she reached up and stroked my cheek.

After too long an interlude, Nolan politely coughed. "I don't know if this helps, but I wasn't able to turn up anything on Derek in either the FBI or NCIC files."

With everything else that had transpired during the past week, I had completely forgotten Nolan's earlier promise to check out Derek's background. "You went ahead with that query anyway?" I asked in amazement. "Even after Derek's death?"

Nolan nodded. "I couldn't see where it would hurt anything. And who knows? We might have got lucky."

"Lucky how?" I asked in confusion.

He shrugged. "It might have showed that Derek had been a serial killer, a rapist, or a pedophile."

I was startled. "Are you serious?"

Nolan grinned. "Not really, but aren't you glad the report came back clean?"

"I suppose so," I answered, shaking my head at the notion. Sometimes Nolan's thought processes were even more convoluted than mine.

"So tell me," he continued, "now that the local gendarmes are finally investigating, when do you think you'll hear back from Pitkin?"

I stood up. "I'll have to call him, I'm sure," I said, laughing. "I doubt if he will ever willingly contact me again."

As it turned out, that prediction proved false. Three days later, a little after ten o'clock in the morning, Pitkin showed up unannounced at my front door. Lee, not yet off to her Manhattan office, escorted the detective into the living room, where I sat reading the latest Jazz Jasper safari mystery by Karin McQuillan, with Bootsie snuggled sleepily around my feet. Uncharacteristically, the dog merely pounded her tail against the floor as the only acknowledgment of Pitkin's entrance.

"I'm sorry to drop in on you like this, Mr. Malachi, Mrs. Malachi," Pitkin explained, nodding to both me and Lee in turn, "but I thought it best to bring you this news in person."

Bootsie wasn't the only one behaving out of character this morning. Was Pitkin actually expressing concern for other people's feelings? I supposed stranger things had been known to happen. Like Rabin embracing Arafat. But I remained guardedly suspicious.

"You remember I told you the autopsy showed that the cause of death was digitoxin poisoning," he continued, accepting Lee's gestured invitation to take a seat on the sofa.

I nodded, I guess still too stunned with his demeanor for speech.

"We conducted a thorough search of Derek's motel room, removed his personal belongings, and ran routine tests on a number of items. Admittedly, with little expectation of finding anything."

Pitkin paused.

"And?" I prodded.

"There was a bottle of vitamins," he finally answered. I felt the pulse beat in the nub on my left thumb. "Twenty or so of these newfangled liquid gel-cap kind of thingamabobs remained in what had originally been a container of fifty."

Pitkin paused again. Irritated with the prolonged explanation, I leaned forward in my chair. "So?" I demanded.

"I guess the killer wasn't taking any chances," Pitkin said. "The lab found lethal concentrations of digitoxin in three of the remaining capsules."

I sat there unmoving, striking a pose of what I'm sure looked to Pitkin like reflective silence, but which merely concealed the awful churning in my stomach. Lee, who had remained standing, suddenly slumped against the arm of my chair.

"We don't yet know how the tampering occurred," the detective continued. "And I doubt that the killer felt any concern that the capsules would ever be examined. After all, digitoxin poisoning would in most circumstances"—and here he had the good grace to blush slightly—"be diagnosed as a heart attack."

I finally found my voice. "Why poison four capsules when one was quite enough?"

Pitkin shook his head. "The only explanation I can come up with is that the killer wanted Derek dead fast." The detective rose to his feet. "These were multiple vitamins that are normally taken once a day, and we obviously don't know how long Derek's luck held out. It would certainly narrow the time frame if we knew how many capsules had been in the bottle at the time of the tampering."

"Four capsules," I whispered, still in disbelief.

"If Derek wasn't consistent about taking his vitamins, and

even the most reliable people will forget from time to time," Pitkin amended, "then we have no way of pinpointing how long ago the killer acted. And people don't always follow the bottle directions. Derek might have doubled up on the dose, or even tripled it. Who knows?"

The killer knew. That was the silent answer I provided to the detective's rhetorical question. I dislodged Bootsie's bulk from around my feet and stood up.

"Can you provide any information about Derek's movements prior to the time he first visited you?" Pitkin asked, edging toward the door.

I shook my head. "No, not a thing, I'm afraid."

"I tried to contact the Louisville police—"

I interrupted. "The Louisville police?"

Pitkin nodded. "Derek's from Louisville. I thought you knew?"

How could I admit to this man that at this particular moment he knew more about my brother than I did? I shook my head again.

"Well, I didn't have much success, I'm afraid," Pitkin explained. "I was told someone in authority would be back in touch, but, as yet, I still haven't heard from anybody. I also tried Derek's home phone, but all I got was his answering machine. But I promise you we'll continue to do everything we can to solve this case." Pitkin stopped in the front entryway. "And please, let us handle it," he added with emphasis.

I nodded. There was no reason to share my plan with the Tipton police.

"If you're finished with Derek's things," I asked meekly, opening the door for his exit, "would it be possible for me to have them?"

Unaware of the ulterior motive behind my request, Pitkin readily agreed. "I'll have them sent over this afternoon," he said. "All except the vitamins, of course," he added with a laugh.

"Is there any reason why I can't have the bottle and the vitamins that weren't tampered with?"

"Why?"

"I'd just like to see what they look like."

"Sounds crazy to me." Pitkin nodded acquiescence, eager, I was positive, to be done with this lunatic citizen.

I closed the door behind him. His true personality had reemerged with that last crack. But I didn't care. I knew what I had to do. And who I had to tell.

Lee walked up beside me, draping her right hand over my left arm.

"Oh, Kyle," she said softly, "I'm so sorry. It seems your brother really had a ruthless enemy. But the police will get to the bottom of it."

I followed her into the kitchen, watching as she began the routine preparations for our lunch. I finally summoned up my courage.

"I'm not waiting on the police," I said.

Lee closed the refrigerator door, her hand holding a head of lettuce.

"What do you mean?" she asked warily. "You're not planning to do something stupid, are you?"

"It depends on what you call stupid."

She dropped the lettuce into the sink, turned on the water, and began pulling apart the leaves. "Knowing you, anything would be stupid."

"I owe it to Derek to try."

"Try what?" she demanded suspiciously. "Just what makes you think you can do any better than the police?" Lee picked the loose leaves out of the sink, placed them in the salad drainer, and snapped the lid in place.

"Because I know something they don't," I answered. I stepped out of harm's way as my wife activated the drying mechanism. If the top was not properly secured, lettuce would go flying across the room. Believe me, I know from personal experience.

"And what's that?" Lee asked, pulling the lid off the container.

"That the killer will try again."

Lee turned in stunned surprise. "Now what makes you say that?"

"He has to," I said, munching on a clean and dry lettuce leaf, then added quietly, "especially when he realizes that Derek Winslow is still alive."

CHAPTER 7

"The reader
is left wondering
which life hangs in the balance—
the old one
or the new one?"

—Stokes Moran,

on Nancy Pickard's *But I Wouldn't Want to Die There*

I needed a pit stop.

I pulled Derek's red Mustang convertible into one of the many empty parking spaces of the Ohio State Visitors' Center, just off Interstate 80 about one mile beyond the Pennsylvania state line.

I looked at my watch. The unfamiliar digital numbers flashed 2:43. Mid-afternoon. I had been on the road for over eight hours, driving, except for one gas refill, virtually non-stop across the interminable length of the Quaker State, and had consumed nothing more than a bag of chips and a Chocolate Soldier since breakfast. I figured I had already logged over four hundred miles and was still only halfway to my destination. At this rate I wouldn't arrive in Louisville until somewhere after eleven tonight. I decided it was time to pick up the pace, even if it meant bending some speed laws.

Then make this quick, I thought, as I pushed my aching body out of the car, sleeping muscles screaming against the sudden movement. I groaned, then Lee's voice echoed in my mind. *You have only yourself to blame,* I heard her say, *I tried to stop you.*

And boy, had she tried, I'll give her that, maintaining an almost constant harangue for the twenty or so hours leading up to my morning departure. From the moment I told her of my intentions, Lee had immediately canceled her impending trip into Manhattan and had constructed every conceivable argument known to man. Or, in her case, woman.

"What about your reviews?" she had demanded. "You've got deadlines to meet."

"Last week, while you were off in Manhattan," I had explained patiently, "I finished off three books and faxed the reviews to the distributor. Those will take me through the end of the month."

"Then what about *Alias Stokes Moran?*"

"I sent the last of my revisions to the publisher two days ago. The next time I'll be needed in the process will be when the author's galleys come in, and my editor told me those aren't likely to arrive until sometime in July."

Lee had frowned. To her credit, though, she fired one last volley. "Well, don't forget about your own mystery novel. You really ought not to take a break when you're this close to the end."

"Not to worry," I had assured her, perhaps somewhat too smugly. "I sketched out the last chapter yesterday morning. All I've got left to do on it is some fleshing out and adding just a few finishing touches."

Lee had temporarily run out of ammunition. But I knew it was just a matter of time before she would reload and come at me again.

Predictably, that moment was not long in arriving. In fact, it occurred only a few minutes later, when Derek's belongings had finally been delivered. I don't know if it was the orphaned look of the items—the single suitcase, the crumpled paper sack, the shiny red automobile—or the forlorn finality of Derek's fate, but Lee's objections suddenly verged on hysteria.

"Kyle, you can't do this," she protested, after I had dutifully signed the requisite paperwork the uniformed policewoman had produced. I pocketed the car keys, picked up the suitcase and the sack, and walked back inside the house.

"I won't let you do this," Lee continued, following right at my heels. "This madman's already killed once. You don't know what you're getting yourself into, and you're going in blind. You don't know who your enemy is, or where the danger may lie. You'll be a sitting duck."

I had given up trying to convince my wife of the inevitability of my decision, so I just opened up the sack and spilled its contents out across the top of the cocktail table.

Here lay Derek's life—a billfold, a watch, a ring, some loose change, a lighter, a pack of cigarettes, the bottle of vitamins. I assumed that the other travel essentials—clothes, shoes, toiletries—were packed away in the suitcase. I'd know soon enough, since I intended to wear those same clothes and carry that same suitcase back into Derek's world.

And just where was that world? All Pitkin had said was Louisville. It was about time I found out the details. I flipped open the billfold and pulled out Derek's driver's license. My brother's address was, as expected, Louisville, Kentucky— 3 River Alley. Wherever, whatever the hell that was, I'd have to get used to it—it was now my home and would remain so for the foreseeable future.

Alone. Without Lee.

"I think the primary reason you're so upset is because you can't go with me," I said gently. "You know this is something I have to do on my own."

"I'm upset because you could get yourself killed," Lee said. "Kyle, I'm just now getting used to being married. I'll never forgive you if you make me a widow." She managed a smile.

"Believe me, that's not something I want either." I continued my search through Derek's billfold. Three credit cards, a telephone calling card, a library card, a membership card for some video rental club, and eighty-seven dollars in cash. No photos. No notes. Nothing at all personal that would give me any clue about the kind of life my brother had lived. Lee was right—I would be going in blind.

"Did you find anything interesting?" Lee asked as I stuffed the cash and cards back in the billfold.

I shook my head. "Not a thing," I admitted, turning my attention to the suitcase.

"Maybe there's something in there," she said optimistically as I unzipped the bag. But a quick frisk through the contents added nothing to the meager information I already had.

"All I've learned is that he lived in Louisville, Kentucky," I said, closing the suitcase. "It's odd that there's nothing personal in any of his belongings. You'd think there'd be notes, or phone numbers, or photos, or something, wouldn't you?"

Lee nodded, then, suddenly animated, said, "You don't think the killer removed all that stuff, do you?"

I shook my head. "I don't see how. Or why, for that matter." I considered the possibility. "The killer would have no idea when Derek would take the poisoned capsule, and I can't see him following Derek around for days and days waiting for it to happen." I reached for the bottle of vitamins, twisted open its plastic lid, and rolled one of the capsules out into my palm. What a nondescript method of murder, I thought. "No, the killer was patient, satisfied that sooner or later Derek would take one of those vitamins. So the absence of anything personal must simply be consistent with Derek's personality. Which is something I'll soon discover."

I stood up, cradling the suitcase in my arms. "I'm going to wash these clothes, get them ready for tomorrow, then I'm going out to check Derek's car. Maybe I'll find something interesting in it." I started toward the kitchen.

As if controlled by a delayed timer, Lee suddenly exploded. "Tomorrow? You don't mean you're leaving so soon?"

I turned at the entrance to the kitchen. "Yes. Too many days have already gone by. Almost two weeks, as a matter of fact, since Derek first appeared on our doorstep. The killer probably thinks he's succeeded. It's time for Derek to reappear."

"And just what do you think the killer will do then?" Lee asked sarcastically. "Give you a medal?"

"With any luck, he might just give himself away."

"Don't you bet on it," Lee called as I headed toward the washing machine.

"Don't you bet against it," I yelled back.

On my way out of the Visitors' Center, I spied a sandwich vending machine. Quicker than stopping for dinner, I reminded myself.

Grasping a processed ham and cheese on rye in one hand and a freezing cola in the other, I hurried back to my car. Derek's car.

I glanced at my watch. Derek's watch. The stopover had cost me less than ten minutes. I backed the Mustang out of the parking lot. I was back on the interstate and heading west toward an eventual rendezvous with I-71, and it still wasn't even 3 P.M. I wondered what my wife was doing.

Last night had been bad, this morning had been worse.

As the afternoon had merged into evening, Lee had stopped speaking to me entirely. She stayed busy, performing meaningless chores, chores she never does—dusting, vacuuming, scrubbing the kitchen floor—occasionally playing with Bootsie, all the while pretending I wasn't there. Playing silent martyr, that was her new role.

I used the time of Lee's cold shoulder routine to prepare for my new role as well. From this point on, I would have to be Derek—talk like Derek, act like Derek, think like Derek.

I doubted I'd have any trouble imitating Derek's slight southern accent. The difference in tone was so minuscule that if anyone questioned it I'd just say I had caught a mild cold on my recent trip. I knew the physical resemblance between us was strong enough to fool just about anybody. After all, Derek had momentarily fooled Lee when he had first come to the door. No, the main problems would probably come with the little unexpected things that could so easily trip me up. Things that, at the moment, I could not predict.

I had so little knowledge about my brother and his life that the prospect of impersonating him truly frightened me. Best not to confide that fear to Lee, however. I needed help, some sort of guide, a possible blueprint.

Dick Francis suddenly came to mind. In *Straight*, Francis had written about a man becoming enmeshed in the life of his dead brother. But those brothers had not been identical twins, had not even been the same age, if I remembered correctly. Suddenly, I recalled the name of the surviving brother—it had been Derek. Derek who had assumed the mantle of his brother Greville. Strange coincidence, I thought. But did I retain any recollection from that book that would assist me now? I couldn't think of any.

The world of mystery fiction is filled with grand and glorious stories of impersonation; and spy fiction simply would never have existed without them—Helen MacInnes with *Assignment in Brittany*, Mary Stewart with *The Ivy Tree*, and L. P. Davies with *The Shadow Before*, just to name a few. But the story that had been in the back of my mind for days, the single one that seemed to offer the only useful parallels, was Daphne du Maurier's *The Scapegoat*. That hypnotic novel has always remained one of my favorites—how one man can make a difference in the lives of those around him, and how much significance a little kindness can play in any human relationship. I had to remember those lessons as I assumed Derek's life, the people I would find there, and the responsibilities that went along with my impersonation. I must take the role seriously and do my brother proud.

No, I realized books wouldn't help me this time. I would have to find my own way, clear my own path. Hopefully, I would come out of the experience victorious and still in one piece. But there was a killer out there, somewhere, who had a different agenda.

"Better give me your wedding ring," Lee had said this morning as I stowed the suitcase in the Mustang's trunk. "Derek didn't wear one."

Oh my God, I thought, the game hasn't even started and I'm already making mistakes.

"Here." I placed the gold band in Lee's right hand, then closed my hand over hers. "Darling," I started—

Lee cut me off. "And I think Derek wore his ring on the middle finger of his right hand."

I fished in the trouser pocket and pulled out the diamond-studded ring, and placed it on the finger my wife had identified. It slipped on easily, a perfect fit.

"Thanks," I said, bending to kiss her. She mumbled words I couldn't quite hear.

"What did you say?"

Lee tilted her head, looking directly into my eyes. "I said, what if he's married?" she answered defiantly.

I smiled. So that's what's been worrying her. "I don't think he is," I answered. "Remember, he's not the one with the wedding ring. I am."

"But what if you're wrong? Or even if he doesn't have a wife, he could still have a girlfriend. How are you going to handle that?"

I laughed and pulled her into a tight embrace. "I'll plead a headache," I said between kisses.

"That old line never worked with me," she teased, pulling out of my arms.

"I never used it with you."

"Kyle, be careful," she said, suddenly turning serious.

"I will," I promised.

"And call me every day. No, better yet, every hour."

"I'll call you once a day," I promised, opening the driver's door. "Say good-bye to Bootsie for me. Where is she, by the way?"

"She's sulking upstairs in our bedroom. I saw her when I checked to see if you had left anything. She's upset with you too."

I climbed behind the wheel and pulled the door closed. "Here I am, going off to face who knows what dangers," I kept my tone light, "and the women in my life have abandoned me."

Lee leaned through the open window and kissed my forehead. "We haven't abandoned you, sweetheart. Just don't you abandon us."

"I won't," I promised. I started the engine, shifted into gear, and drove away from my house, leaving behind the safe and sedate world of Kyle Malachi, Lee and Bootsie, Stokes Moran, mystery novels, and nosy next-door neighbors.

For better or worse, I was now Derek Winslow, and there was no turning back.

CHAPTER 8

"The dichotomy
of the dual personality
is fascinating,
the juggling act of keeping
the identities separate amazing,
and the anguish
at the heart of each character
undisguisable."

—Stokes Moran, on Natasha Cooper's *Poison Flowers*

I entered the Louisville city limits at 9:33, not exactly the shank of the evening, but earlier than I had anticipated. The May sun had only been absent from the starless sky for little more than an hour, but it was dark as only a burgeoning pre-summer night can be.

I was nearly out of gas, both figuratively and literally. At the first opportunity, I exited the interstate, now displaying the sub-urban girth of a Los Angeles freeway, desperate for a pump of any kind. The needle on the Mustang's fuel gauge had dropped below "E" some twenty miles back, and both the car and I had been coasting on hope for the last fifteen minutes.

I spotted a Chevron station up ahead on the right, guided the Mustang to a full-service berth, and killed the engine. I instructed the female attendant to fill the tank, check the oil, and wash the windshield. While she was busily engaged with those activities, I went inside the kiosk in search of a city map.

"Know where River Alley is?" I asked the obese woman behind the counter.

"Ain't never heard of it," she answered. "Suppose to be here in Louisville?"

"Yep," I said, acquainting the taste of Derek's southern twang to my tongue. "Let me have one of them maps over there." Don't overdo it, I thought.

The clerk reached behind her and pulled out a Louisville street map.

"Be three dollars and nineteen cents," she said, sliding the map across the counter.

"Add that to the gas the girl's pumping."

I unfolded the map and found the index. I scanned down the entries. No River Alley. Oh boy.

"There's no River Alley listed," I complained.

The lady frowned. "Do you know the zip code?"

I told her. "That's downtown," she said. "Take River Road here till you get to Second Street. River Alley should be down there somewheres."

"Where's River Road?"

"Next light up. Total's twenty-six fifty-seven," she said, reading from a digital display underneath the counter.

I lifted two twenties from Derek's billfold, waited for the change, and thanked the clerk.

She nodded. "But don't get on the Second Street bridge," she cautioned, "or you'll be in Indiana before you have a chance to turn around."

I thanked her a second time, walked out through the door, smiled another thank-you to the attendant, and climbed behind the Mustang's steering wheel. Consulting the map for River Road, I found it intersected with Second Street.

At the next traffic light, I turned left.

Twenty blocks later I discovered that the clerk didn't know Louisville any better than I could read a map. River Road never does meet Second Street. I could see Second Street above me, but it was one of those predicaments where you can't get there from here. Then I got lucky. In a frantic effort to connect with Second Street, I made a number of confused turns that eventually landed me on a side street near the river where I just happened to spot a sign proclaiming River Alley. And it wasn't really even an alley, just a narrow strip of asphalt between two huge warehouses.

I headed the Mustang down the darkened alley. The place gave me the willies. No streetlamps. No doorways. No room to park. Strange place for Derek to live, I concluded.

If I had the right address, I thought dejectedly. I glanced at my watch. The dial glowed 10:02, too late to be out exploring, especially in this isolated part of town. The alley dead-ended into an embankment; I shifted the car into reverse and looked again for a possible entryway.

The two buildings seemed to be virtually identical in size, shape, and design, with the only breaks in the solid brick structures coming at the docking bays, both of which appeared to be closed up tight. If Derek had lived in one of these buildings, then which one? And how could I identify it without putting myself at risk?

I switched on the Mustang's interior light, intending to take another look at the map, but instead I noticed something on the driver's visor that should have registered with me much sooner. An automatic garage-door opener.

I slipped the mechanism off its hook and aimed the device at the loading dock on my left. Nothing happened. I tried the same maneuver again on my right. Miraculously, the big door started to grind ponderously upward. As soon as I judged there was sufficient clearance for the Mustang, I eased the car into the cavernous opening.

This part of the warehouse had obviously been converted into a makeshift parking garage. Three cars and one van occupied four of the six marked slots. The two empty spaces were both on the far left end of the structure. I slipped the Mustang into the one next to the wall and killed the engine.

The big door noisily reached its zenith, paused for a minute, then jerkily started back down. Fluorescent lights burned in the corners of the garage. Either they stayed on continuously or else a timer controlled the length of their illumination. If the latter proved to be the case, I could be stranded in total darkness in a matter of minutes, or even seconds. I opened the car door, careful not to scrape the paint against the stone wall, sidled through the narrow passage, and grabbed Derek's suitcase out of the trunk. Then I looked for an exit.

Three possibilities loomed before me. A stairwell in the middle of the bay led up approximately ten feet to a gray steel door with a yard-high number 1 boldly emblazoned in yellow. To my right, another stairwell spiderwebbed some thirty feet up the far wall to a door similarly marked 2. But not five steps from where I now stood, a third stairwell spiraled up a dizzying fifty feet to a door where the distant 3 appeared minuscule in comparison to the other numbers.

I craned my neck. So that's 3 River Alley. Just my luck, I swore irritably—Derek must have been part mountain goat to have lived in a place like this. With thoughts of Jimmy Stewart and *Vertigo* dogging my every step, I carefully scaled the daunting obstacle, praying that the lights would not suddenly go out and leave me hanging precariously in midair.

Breathlessly, I topped the final riser. Now what? I thought. I fished Derek's keys out of my pants pocket. In addition to the trunk and ignition keys, the ring held two other keys. I inserted the larger of the two into the door lock and turned. Nothing. Please, I begged as I tried the other key, open the damn door. Thankfully, it did. With a sigh, I pushed against the steel panel and stepped inside.

As soon as I crossed the threshold, the lights behind me went out. But, just as suddenly, other lights came on, accompanied by the sound of rushing water. I was temporarily disoriented, but my confusion only lasted a second. My head cleared quickly, giving me a good opportunity to survey my new surroundings.

It was one huge rectangular room, measuring at least fifty feet across and possibly three times that size in length. I stood near the left-end base of the rectangle. The wall behind me, as well as the two connecting walls, were windowless. But the outside wall, across from where I now stood, contained a solid bank of louvered windows, starting about six inches off the floor and extending at least twenty feet up to where they almost touched the edge of the ceiling. The room reminded me of an airplane hangar, a giant skating rink, or even an indoor football field. Not exactly my idea of a cozy little nest.

"Is anybody here?" I called, the words echoing hollowly in my ears. No response. The place certainly looked deserted, but I thought it best not to take any chances. I called again. When no answer came back this time either, I dropped Derek's suitcase on the floor and closed the door behind me.

The entry area seemed to be the only illuminated part of the room. Here track lighting highlighted what appeared to be a scale reproduction of a tropical rain forest. A floor-to-ceiling latticework supported trailing vines behind which a giant waterfall cascaded down from the ceiling. Bushy ferns and flowering plants surrounded a large reflecting pool, where I spotted several varieties of fish swimming languidly among the rocks. A brick path led through the lush setting and ended where a white wicker divan and two matching chairs were placed strategically at the edge of the pool.

Directing my attention away from this tranquil but unexpected sight, I moved to my right, toward the center of the room. I had taken only half a dozen steps when a new track of lights clicked on, illuminating another portion of the room, while the area I had just left went just as suddenly dark. Ah, I thought, motion detectors.

I suddenly realized that I no longer heard the sound of the waterfall. Nor did I recall hearing it before I had initially crossed the room's threshold. I backtracked, triggering once again the first set of lights. Just as I expected, the waterfall sprang to noisy life. I laughed. Even the waterfall is mechanized, I thought. I headed back toward the center of the room.

Ahead of me, occupying roughly a twenty- by twenty-foot island of prime floor space, sat an enclosed structure. Reaching the entire height of the room, its bottom half had solid walls while the top half sported hanging curtains. A ten-foot ladder was attached to the side I now approached, secured at the floor and ending at the bottom of the flowing teal curtains. Curiosity got the better of me, so I climbed to the top of the ladder and pushed the draperies aside. The interior revealed a fairly normal-looking bedroom—shag-carpeted floor, two nightstands, writing bureau and chair, a walk-in closet, and a king-sized water bed with mirrored headboard situated under a cupolaed skylight. Again, track lighting provided the illumination.

This is one strange setup, I thought, as I edged down the ladder. Once back on the floor, I opened the door in the bottom tier. A bathroom. On the wall perpendicular to the door was a double vanity with a mirror running the entire length of the room. To my left, a curtained cubicle thinly veiled the toilet. A communal shower, with six water spigots visible—reminding me of my college dormitory—took up a good two-thirds of the bathroom. As with a refrigerator, I was certain the track lighting would be extinguished once I closed the door.

Rube Goldberg would have loved this setup, I thought, as I headed toward the far wall. Again, a few steps distant and the lights came on in front of me and disappeared behind me. This is beginning to get on my nerves, I muttered. In the light of day, I promised, I will figure out a way to disable these stupid motion detectors.

The wall ahead showcased the kitchen area. Familiar items were attractively arranged in a utilitarian grouping—refrigerator, stove, microwave, dishwasher, butcher's table, sink, dinette with two chairs.

Suddenly, I felt overwhelmed with fatigue. It had been a long and tiring day, with almost fourteen hours spent on the road. I decided to leave the rest of the exploring for tomorrow morning. All I wanted at the moment was a hot shower and a soft bed.

I tripped the track lighting several times on my subsequent journeys across the room—retrieving Derek's suitcase, stashing his belongings, getting a glass of water—before I finally stood ready to enter the shower.

I was mystified. There were no controls. No hot and cold knobs. I was running out of patience with this nuclear prototype. I stepped into the shower area, thinking perhaps I'd find the answer in there. Suddenly, spray from six jets hit me simultaneously. At first, I jumped, but soon the pulsating water—starting comfortably warm and then gradually increasing in temperature—began to soothe my aching muscles. I spotted a soap canister attached to the near wall, and as I moved toward it, I noticed that the water moved with me. After I lathered up, the jets followed my movement back to the center of the shower. I laughed. I was beginning to like this particular modern marvel.

I felt a slight rush of warm air against my right ear. I turned, startled. A naked man stood in the shower with me.

"Hello, lover," he said, "welcome home."

· · ·

Somehow I managed to get out of that shower without revealing my identity—though, needless to say, that had been about the only thing that hadn't been revealed—or compromising my reputation. Lee, at least, would be happy with the latter.

I had escaped the man's clutches with only a skimpy towel wrapped around my middle. Luckily, I had remembered seeing a terry-cloth bathrobe among Derek's belongings. I climbed the ladder, retrieved the garment from where I had stashed it, and slipped it over my shoulders. I felt a little bit more protected with it sashed tightly about my body.

But right now I had more immediate worries than warding off unwelcome advances. The man would be walking out of that bathroom at any minute, and I had to be mentally prepared to face him.

Who was this guy? Obviously, he was somebody who had known Derek intimately, probably a roommate, or, based on my recent experience in the shower, a partner, or longtime companion. And I couldn't very well come right out and ask his name. Something told me he wasn't a likely candidate as Derek's murderer, but I couldn't know that for sure. I had to remain on guard.

Time. I had to stall for time. The longer I could delay detection, the better my chances at maintaining the facade. If I could somehow make it till morning, I might have a fighting chance for success.

I considered getting into bed and feigning sleep. That would certainly delay any possible conversation. But no, I decided, that idea posed too much of a risk. For one thing, as far as I had determined, there was only the one bed, and the man, whoever he was, would probably climb into the bed with me. Even discounting the sexual ramifications, I just couldn't chance any pillow talk, either tonight or tomorrow morning. No, going to bed was definitely not a viable option.

Then what? Stay up all night? What if the man wanted to talk? I couldn't exactly pretend amnesia.

For the first time, I truly began to appreciate the herculean task I faced. What had I gotten myself into? How could I possibly navigate my way safely through all the potential pitfalls inherent in this wild scheme? It would be a miracle if I pulled off this charade, and I couldn't very well ask any questions. I needed an ally, someone I could trust, who could provide me with the answers I desperately needed. I realized impersonation wasn't as easy as books and movies always made it appear.

I suddenly felt my world start to disintegrate.

Stokes Moran had been problem enough. Lee had claimed I was jealous of my own pseudonym. Then, with the traumatic news of my birth and adoption, I wasn't even sure I knew who Kyle Malachi was anymore. Now I had a third identity I was trying to juggle. Talk about split personality! I would definitely need the counseling of a good psychiatrist when this was all over. If I didn't go completely certifiable before then, that is.

The bathroom door opened, and the man walked out toweling his hair dry and wearing a terry-cloth robe identical to Derek's.

"What got into you in there?" he asked, dropping the towel around his shoulders, then cinching the robe more tightly around his waist. "You usually enjoy our water games."

"I just guess I'm too tired," I stammered.

"Well, the way you bolted out of there, I thought you'd seen a ghost."

"I wasn't expecting you." Boy, was that an understatement! "You startled me."

The man laughed. "You looked like a scalded rat the way you skittered out of there." He walked toward the bank of windows on the opposite side of the room. I followed.

A new set of track lights clicked on, illuminating a sitting area. I had completely overlooked this grouping in my earlier explorations. There was a sectional sofa, upholstered in teal velveteen, and two overstuffed matching chairs, two end tables, and a cocktail table. He sat in one of the chairs, while I settled nervously across from him on one end of the sofa, folding my legs underneath me and tucking the hem of the robe around my knees.

"What are you doing sitting over there?" he demanded.

Such a simple thing as picking a place to sit and I had already made a mistake. "Just felt like it."

"You sure are acting strange tonight." He picked a loose thread from the robe's lapel. "By the way, how was your trip?"

"Oh, fine," I mumbled. What else could I say?

"You were sure gone long enough, and I can't believe you didn't call once in more than two weeks. I ought to be hurt, but I guess that means you came face-to-face with your brother?"

This guy was obviously current on Derek's activities. I reminded myself he was a possible murderer. "Uh-huh," I answered vaguely.

"Well, is that all you've got to say?" He laughed, casually draping one naked leg across the arm of the chair. "As excited as you were a couple of weeks ago, I would have thought that when you finally came face-to-face with your brother, it would have been somewhat on the order of finding the Holy Grail."

I matched his laughter, playing for time. What do I say now? How do I get out of this? Oh well, I decided, why not the truth? "He had trouble adjusting to the news."

"I can imagine."

I decided I'd had enough of this being on the defensive. It was time for me to take the initiative and turn the spotlight away from Derek. "How about you?" I asked. "What have you been up to while I've been gone?"

"You know what I've been doing." I nodded sagely, trying to look knowledgeable. The man lifted a slim silver-plated container from the top of the cocktail table, shook out a cigarette, placed it in his mouth, and reached for a matching silver-plated lighter. "I've been in Chicago."

"When did you get in?" That seemed like a safe and natural question.

"Just a few minutes ago. I decided I needed a break. I've been killing myself over this stupid play for six weeks straight."

Ah, an actor? Or producer? Maybe even a director? But somehow definitely connected with the theater. "Problems?" I prompted.

He laughed. "Not exactly." He exhaled contentedly, then continued his explanation. "When the project first started out, it was going to be a gay parody on Lerner and Loewe—*My Fair Laddie*, Elijah Doolittle, you know the shtick. But the more I got into the character of Higgins, the more I came to realize that, quite by accident, we had hit on the truth. Giving Higgins a romantic interest in Eliza never seemed quite right, but when you change the emphasis from heterosexual to homosexual, it works perfectly. What it means is that *My Fair Lady* was always intended to be a gay story. It's just that nobody—not George Bernard Shaw, not Lerner and Loewe—ever had the courage to present it that way."

I could tell from his animation that here was a man committed to his profession, fervent in his beliefs, comfortable with star billing, alive on center stage. But more than that, simply by listening, I had managed to learn that he was an actor, playing the part of Henry Higgins in a Chicago production. Maybe with a little clever coaxing I could also get him to reveal his name, prodding him with something like "I can see your name up in lights" or "And the winner is . . ." I smiled. Perhaps my subterfuge would succeed after all.

Just then I heard a persistent scratching noise coming from the base of the sofa. Almost instantaneously, a giant rat-looking animal scampered onto my lap. I shrieked, jumped up, and in the process dumped the creature unceremoniously onto the floor.

"Get that thing away from me," I yelled, standing in the middle of the sofa.

The man kneeled down, gently picked the animal up, and cooingly cradled him in his arms. Then he stood up.

"I'm Lowell Dodge," the man said, calmly stroking the animal's fur. "Who the hell are you?"

CHAPTER 9

"Attacking from all sides,
the novel
is basically the story
of one man
becoming entrapped
by the identity of another."

—Stokes Moran, on Dick Francis' *Straight*

"Derek's dead, isn't he?"

Lowell's words—flat, colorless, devoid of any emotion—came just seconds after the little animal had unmasked me.

I nodded.

"How did he die?"

"He was poisoned."

"Intentionally?"

"He was murdered."

"Who?"

"That's what I'm here to find out."

"You're his brother, aren't you?"

Again I nodded.

Lowell walked over to the windows and looked out into the dark night. He stood there several minutes, trying to come to terms, I suppose, with the news of Derek's death. Finally, he turned back toward me and said, still holding the struggling animal against his chest, "This is Weezer. I take her with me everywhere I go. For the past six weeks, she's been with me in Chicago. She enjoyed her little adventure, but now she's happy to be back home, aren't you, Weezer?" He held her up to his face, then turned the squirming creature toward me. "Derek was the one who named her. When we first got her two years ago, he started calling her Weasel. Then, over time, it somehow evolved into Weezer, and the name just sorta stuck."

"What kind of animal is she?" I asked.

"Oh, I'm sorry," he said, "I thought you knew. She's a ferret." He nuzzled his nose against her mottled gray-and-brown fur. "She's just wonderful, and we both adore her. Some ferrets can be quite vicious or have an odor. But we got lucky. She's an absolute pussycat, aren't you, sweetie?" He kissed the tip of her snout.

Abruptly, I said, "Lowell, my name's Kyle. Kyle Malachi."

He vaulted the animal onto his shoulder and stuck out his hand. "Pleased to meet you," he said formally. "Derek told me he had a twin, but—" He stopped in mid-sentence.

"But what?"

"You look just like him."

I didn't know what to say. I felt like an intruder, an impostor. Lowell needed time to assimilate, to adjust, to grieve, and how could he possibly do that as long as I remained in his home? I was a constant visual reminder of the person he had lost.

"I'm going to a hotel," I said decisively. "You don't need me here right now."

Lowell shook his head. "Nonsense," he said. "You must stay. I want you to tell me every detail."

For the next forty-five minutes, that's what I did. I finally ended with the now shattered scenario for trapping Derek's killer.

"But no," he objected excitedly. "Don't give up on it. I think it's a terrific plan. And I'm sure you can pull it off," he insisted, then added with a twisted smile, "with my help, of course."

"That would be wonderful," I admitted honestly. "But don't you think it would be easier on you if I weren't around?"

"Not in the least. As long as you're here, it'll be like Derek's still alive. And anyway," he added with emphasis, "I want to find Derek's killer as badly as you do."

I glanced at my watch. It was now past midnight. Lowell, taking the hint, offered me the use of the sofa and then, when I accepted, went to get bedding. He returned with sheets, pillows, and a comforter.

"I think you'll be fairly comfortable. I've spent a few nights on that couch myself." He grinned mischievously.

"Thank you," I said, spreading the silk sheets over the crushed velveteen.

"Well, I'm going up to bed, then." He started to walk away, then turned back. "Oh, if Weezer tries to get in bed with you, just kick her out. She'll find someplace else."

I laughed. "Is that something she's likely to do?"

Lowell grinned. "With her, you never know. Why do you think Derek and I built that platform for our bedroom?"

"You mean she can't get up there?"

He shook his head. "Climbing ladders is just about the only thing she can't do. At least not yet."

"One other thing," I remembered, "how do I get rid of these blasted lights."

"You don't like them?" He seemed amused.

"I guess I could get used to them."

He laughed. "Don't worry. I'll take care of them for you. Good night."

As exhausted as I was, I felt I'd be dead to the world as soon as my head hit the pillow. But for some reason, I just couldn't fall asleep that night. Two hours later, lying alone in the dark, I was still reliving the day's events.

Tomorrow, I knew, the picture that had been my brother's life would come more clearly into focus. But I had learned a good deal about him already—the most unexpected news, I suppose, was that he had been gay. How significant a fact was that? And could it conceivably have anything to do with his death?

I suppose here finally was a possible indication that homosexuality was a product of environment and not heredity. The closest relationship in nature—identical twins. Yet I was straight, and he had been gay. Why? What had made us different in that one respect when in so many other ways we had been so alike? Was it simply a matter of choice, after all? Or were there other factors at play as well? Factors that perhaps blinded me to their significance. Was sexual preference not a definite, but something that simply existed on a sliding scale, with one extreme defined as straight and the other as gay? I certainly didn't know the answer, and admittedly my insight in this area was limited.

I did know, though, that both men and women had found me attractive over the years. Standing almost six feet, weighing only a little over a hundred and fifty pounds, with a pleasing visage, sandy-blond hair, and green eyes, I was well aware of the favorable impression I made. Was it only my naiveté, my inexperience, that tilted me toward the heterosexual side of human behavior?

I found I liked Lowell Dodge. I also found it difficult to accept that he had had anything to do with Derek's murder. But I had to remember that many times killers lurked behind smiling faces. The least likely suspect, and all that.

Lowell Dodge. More attractive really than Derek. Than me. Taller by an inch or two, blessed with a swimmer's build and dark brown hair and eyes, Lowell possessed the confident bearing and assured elegance of a professional model. I could understand how Derek had connected with him. If I were a different sort, I could see how easy it would be for me to slip into his bed and console his grief with my Derek-like body, to delay the finality of Derek's absence from his life for one night longer. But that would have been a betrayal of Derek, by both Lowell and me. Not to mention, if I had been so inclined, how Lee would have reacted to something like that. Lee!

"Dammit." I bolted upright on the sofa, the sheets tangled around me. "I forgot to call Lee."

As worried as she had been, my wife would absolutely kill me for not calling! I looked at the luminous digits on Derek's watch: 2:14. It was certainly too late to call tonight, even if I had any inkling where in this huge barn Lowell kept the phone.

I eased back against the pillows. Well, calling Lee would just have to be one more thing left for tomorrow. Like learning more about my brother's life, like understanding where I go from here, like figuring out how to control these stupid lights.

And, of course, like finding out who killed my brother.

"Tell me everything you know about Derek," I said. "Don't leave anything out."

Lowell laughed. "You got twelve years? That's how long we were together."

We sat at the breakfast table, nursing our third cups of coffee. The morning light, streaming in through the wall of windows, had somewhat diminished for me the gargantuan aspects of the room. Still, I remained in awe of its size, and especially of the panoramic view its fifty-foot height provided of the Ohio River, which could be seen just the other side of the glass. I had admired the view in detail during my call to Lee just thirty minutes earlier. As I had predicted, she was not exactly the soul of understanding.

"Don't ever do anything like this to me again!" she warned, after she had first determined that all was well. "I was just about ready to call out the National Guard."

With my life and marriage under dire threat, I promised that I would telephone her each morning at precisely eight o'clock. On the dot. Not a minute later.

"Remember, you don't know who the killer might be, so

be on your guard every second," she cautioned as we ended the conversation. "And please watch everything you eat and drink."

"More coffee?" Lowell offered, the steaming carafe poised expectantly over my mug. This guy a poisoner? I found it impossible to believe. Had he intended anything more sinister than an overdose of caffeine, I would already be a goner. Declining, I shook my head. "I'm already two cups over my limit."

"Me too," he answered laughingly, then proceeded to top off his mug.

"Where's the ferret this morning?" I wondered why I had not yet seen the furry little animal.

"Oh, she's probably curled up asleep somewhere."

"You mean you don't know where she is?"

Lowell added a dollop of cream to his coffee. "She has a couple of favorite hiding places, and I can usually find her when I need to. Don't worry. She'll make an appearance when she gets hungry enough."

It seemed to me that such a tiny creature could easily disappear forever in this immense arena, but then what did I know?

"Tell me about Derek," I repeated, once he had stirred in more sugar.

"I met Derek when I was twenty-two," Lowell began. "He was doing a behind-the-scenes story on the local modeling scene."

"A story?"

"Yes. At the time, Derek was still a reporter with the *Louisville Courier.*"

"A reporter?"

"Yes, didn't you know?"

I shook my head. "I don't know anything about my brother."

"Derek was this city's best investigative reporter," Lowell said proudly. "He even won a 1980 Pulitzer Prize for a series he did on toxic dumping in the Cumberland River."

Derek a reporter? A writer? I never would have guessed.

"The modeling piece was just a routine assignment, but it did bring us together." He smiled. "You've heard of sparks flying? Well, that's how it was for us from the very first moment." His face clouded, and he abruptly stopped speaking.

"Are you a model?" I asked after a minute's silence.

"I was then." As suddenly as Lowell had shut down, that was just how quickly he bounced back. "I did newspaper layouts and television shoots for Merkel's, a department store here in Louisville. Dress clothes. Cologne. Underwear. That kind of stuff."

"You didn't like modeling?"

He laughed. "I was only doing it to piss off my father."

"Your father?"

"Yeah. Lowell Dodge the Third." He intoned capital letters. "Louisville aristocracy. According to him, I had a social stature to maintain, and modeling was not in his game plan. He wanted me to go to law school."

"So what happened when you met Derek?"

"For one thing, Derek forced me to realize that making my father miserable—while that might be one hell of a lot of fun—still need not be my life's sole ambition."

"How did your father get along with Derek?"

Lowell laughed. "Father never acknowledged Derek's existence. Of course, he never really had to. He died of a heart attack just weeks after Derek and I met."

I frowned. Scratch off the best suspect I'd thus far heard about.

"So you gave up modeling and Derek gave up reporting?"

He nodded. "But not in the cut-and-dried manner you described. I continued to model for a couple years more, then turned my interest toward the theater. Derek, on the other hand, stayed with the newspaper until two years ago."

"What made him give it up?"

"He said he was getting too old for the late hours, that his type of reporting was really a young man's game. But I think he had just gotten burned out. After all, he had been at it for almost two decades."

"What did he do then?"

"Went freelance. Sold his talents to the highest bidder."

"Was he successful?"

"Oh sure." Lowell grinned. "You have to remember Derek Winslow was something of a local celebrity. His byline had been well known for years, so he didn't have any trouble finding clients."

"What kind of jobs did he take?"

"Mostly puff pieces."

"Puff pieces?" I didn't recognize the term.

"You know, CEO profiles for corporate annual reports. That kind of thing."

I nodded my understanding. "What was he working on lately?"

"Just after I left for Chicago, Derek accepted a commission from the Holcomb Company."

"I think I've heard of it."

"You should." Lowell laughed. "It's one of the largest privately held companies in the United States, with gross revenues of more than seven billion dollars last year alone."

Now it was my turn to laugh. "How do you know that?" I asked, amazed.

"Derek always shared his research with me."

"But you were in Chicago." My suspicions about Lowell hadn't completely disappeared.

"There's a great little invention you might be aware of. It's called a telephone, I believe. Ever heard of it?"

"All right." I grinned. "I guess I deserved that."

Lowell suddenly frowned. "You know, now that I think about it, that was the only time he really said anything at all about the Holcomb Company."

"Is that significant?"

"I don't know. We kept missing each other's calls. I'd leave messages on his answering machine, and he'd do likewise on mine. I was so caught up in working on the show that it didn't strike me as odd until right this minute, but in the last six weeks Derek and I actually only talked together twice."

"Then it was at the time of the second call when he told you he had found his brother," I said. "Found me," I amended.

"That's right," Lowell confirmed, standing at the window and looking out over the river. "He was real excited about that."

"Had he been searching a long time?" I swallowed the last cold dregs of coffee and joined Lowell at the window.

"You know, it's strange," Lowell said wistfully, "but Derek hadn't talked about his adoption in years. When we first got together, it was a subject that just about preoccupied his every waking thought. He wanted family, he wanted to connect. But, over the years, it sorta stopped being so all-important to him. I guess maybe the reason for that was that he felt he had finally found his sense of family with me."

Family. I was Derek's family, but I had denied the connection until it was too late. Beyond the window to my right, I idly observed the cars crossing the massive steel bridge that spanned the river, the drivers impatient to get to their offices, like worker ants scurrying to their nesting hills. Fighting rush hour traffic, schedules to maintain, promises to keep. A daily routine. Normal people, normal lives.

"Had Derek always known he was adopted?" I finally asked, squinting against the glaring sun that shimmered off the water's surface and slowly burned away the last remnants of early-morning fog.

I caught Lowell's nod out of the corner of my eye. "He lived in an orphanage until he was four. Then a nice couple adopted him."

"What were they like?"

"I don't know. I never met them. They were killed in a car crash when Derek was in college."

Strange the parallels I shared with Derek. My parents had also died while I was in college—first my mother had been claimed by cancer, then a few short months later my father had taken his own life. Ironically, the two sets of adoptive parents had been removed from each of our lives—Derek's and mine—at possibly the same time, the circumstances certainly different but the devastation, the loss, must surely have been similar. Coincidence? Circles within circles?

"How much of his true background did Derek know?"

"Hardly anything," Lowell answered, turning to face me. "All he knew was that he had been abandoned as an infant. The story he used to tell was that he had been found on the steps of a church, a note giving his name and explaining that he was an orphan who needed a good home."

"Then Derek Winslow was his real name?"

"I'm sorry." Lowell shook his head. "I should have made that clearer. Winslow was the name of his adoptive parents. It was only Derek's first name that was mentioned in the note."

"So the Winslows let him keep his given name?"

"That's right. After all, he was already four years old, and his name was about the only thing he had that he could call his own."

Derek. But Derek who?

Then—Kyle? I now seriously questioned whether I had always been a Kyle. Given the lifelong secrecy surrounding my adoption, I doubted that my parents would have risked keeping my birth name.

"Do you have any idea what could have got Derek interested in his adoption again?" My eyes met Lowell's. He shook his head.

"Whatever it was," he answered, "it happened in the last six weeks, while I was away in Chicago. As I said, it had been a subject Derek had all but forgotten over the past few years."

"Could there be a connection with the Holcomb Company?"

"That's certainly logical. After all, that was his current project. Like I told you, Derek was a top investigative reporter, and he still had those skills even if he no longer routinely used them. Maybe he came across something that only he would recognize as significant."

I ran my hands impatiently through my hair. "But how will we ever find out?"

Lowell smiled. "That's easy. We just check his diary."

"Diary? Derek kept a diary?"

"Sure." Lowell nodded. "Derek started a fresh one with every new job. He wanted a precise record of everything he did—his time, his research, his expenses. He said he did it in case the client or the IRS ever had questions, but I think it was more a habit he picked up from his newspaper days. He made notes about everything, even personal stuff such as his next doctor's appointment or items he wanted to pick up at the supermarket. You know, things like that. I'm sure we'll find the answers to all our questions in there."

"Where's the diary now?" I asked eagerly.

"Don't you have it? Derek always kept it with him."

I shook my head decisively. "I have everything he brought with him to Connecticut. And believe me, there was no diary. I would have noticed."

"If Derek didn't have it with him, then it has to be here." Lowell walked halfway across the room to a cluster of furniture I had missed the previous night. Even from my distant perspective, I could identify a desk, a table, a chair, a computer terminal, a printer, and two other items that were probably a modem and a fax machine. Lowell ransacked through the desk drawers for several minutes, then returned empty-handed.

"It's not with his other diaries. That means Derek had to have kept it with him."

I frowned. "But I told you it wasn't among his effects. Can't you think of any other place it could be?"

"If the diary were here, it would be in the desk. Derek was nothing if not methodical. He was fanatical about there being a place for everything, and everything in its place." Lowell paused, then suggested, "Maybe the killer took it."

"I doubt it. In all likelihood, the killer was probably hundreds of miles away when Derek took the fatal vitamin."

Lowell frowned. "Vitamin?"

"Yeah, somebody put poison in four of Derek's vitamins. I guess the killer wasn't taking any chances."

Lowell laughed and shook his head. "That's crazy."

"Of course it's crazy. Murder always is."

I noted the puzzled expression that haunted Lowell's face. "That's not what you meant, though, is it?"

He shook his head. "No. It's the vitamins. That's the crazy thing."

"Why is that crazy?"

"Because Derek didn't believe in vitamins, and he never took a single vitamin a day in his life."

CHAPTER 10

"Threading his way
among land mines
that could explode in his face
at any minute,
the author
makes it safely
across his narrative field."

—Stokes Moran,

on Mark Richard Zubro's *A Simple Suburban Murder*

$\mathcal{T}$he Free Public Library is located on West York Street in downtown Louisville, only a short drive from Derek's loft—"loft" being the preferred word of choice over the more mundane "apartment" or the basically inaccurate "condo," as Lowell had considerately pointed out while we were still dissecting Derek's character.

"Derek loved the loft," Lowell said after he had given me directions to the library. "He was the one who first envisioned it as a series of separate components, individual environments complete within themselves."

Lowell laughed. "Derek liked the loft's privacy, but what I

think I most like about it is the feeling of security it gives me. With the lighting controlled by pressure sensors in the floor"—ah, not motion detectors at all—"no one ever arrives unannounced."

"But why doesn't Weezer set them off?"

"They're set for one hundred pounds. Weezer, at a pound and a half, barely registers."

Then we had segued from the topic of interior design to a lengthy and animated discussion about the two obvious conflicts Lowell's recollections had unearthed.

"Maybe I didn't know him as well as I thought," Lowell had confided at one point.

"No, I don't think that's it," I answered. "You were in Chicago; there was no way you could know what was going on in his mind. Seemingly by chance he stumbled on something to do with his adoption, and for some reason he changes his behavior. Why?" I pounded my right fist in my left hand. "There has to be a reason, a connection."

"I still don't understand how you can be so certain the killer didn't take the diary," Lowell said.

"I've read a lot of mystery novels"—now was not the time to explain how I made my living—"and it just doesn't follow that the villain would plant a time bomb and then stick around for it to go off."

"What are you talking about?"

"The vitamins."

"I thought we were talking about the diary."

I nodded. "Follow me in this for a second, okay? If the killer took the diary, then that makes the diary a possible motive for Derek's murder. Right? After all, why take the diary otherwise?"

"I suppose." Lowell agreed without much enthusiasm.

"Then it stands to reason that the killer would not risk taking it until after Derek's death."

Lowell shook his head in confusion. "I don't follow you on that one at all. Why couldn't the killer have swiped it, say, a week earlier?"

"Because, then, Derek would have been able to reconstruct it."

"What difference does that make?"

"Don't you see, if the diary is important enough for the killer to steal, then it has to be stolen when Derek can't recreate it. In other words, it has to be taken after he's dead."

"Let's say I accept your reasoning." But Lowell's skeptical tone gave the lie to his words. "So what's to prevent the killer from doing just that—taking the diary after Derek's death?"

"The method of murder prevents the killer from doing just that," I mimicked. "If the killer had shot Derek or stabbed him or strangled him, yes, then I'd say the killer took the diary. But Derek wasn't killed face-to-face—he was poisoned. The killer could have been, and probably was, several states away when it happened."

"So what's your point?"

"It's simple," I said patiently. "The killer does not have the diary."

"Then where is it?"

"It's wherever Derek put it."

Lowell threw his hands up into the air. "I told you Derek always kept the diary with him."

I shook my head. "Then Derek changed his habits. With both the diary and the vitamins."

"Not again with the vitamins," Lowell said impatiently.

"He was not forced to take them."

"How do you know?"

This time I lifted my hands. "What's the purpose? A killer wouldn't go to all the trouble to doctor four vitamin capsules and then physically force-feed his victim the poison. It doesn't make sense."

"Then what do you think happened?"

"I think that Derek intentionally left the diary someplace and that he also willingly took the vitamins."

"But why?" Lowell moaned. "Why, when both acts were so out of character for him?"

"If we knew that, then I think we'd probably know everything."

Constructed in the French Renaissance style popular with turn-of-the-century American bureaucrats, the Louisville library, according to Lowell, was the one absolute constant in Derek's professional routine. No matter what the assignment, Derek always began his research at this two-story T-shaped building in the heart of downtown. It seemed feasible that if we carefully followed Derek's routine, we just might discover the same information that had eventually led him to me. That, at least, was Lowell's theory. And he had also explained why I should be the one to go to the library.

"They'll think you're Derek. It will make it a lot easier to get their cooperation."

So, while Lowell was off on some mysterious errands of his own, I found myself once again impersonating my brother.

"Good morning," I said to the auburn-haired receptionist who stood behind the information desk.

"Good morning, Derek," she answered.

Now what do I say? "I wonder," I started, "if you could get me the material I was working on the last time I was here?" That request echoed stupidly in my ears, and I was convinced the receptionist would easily see through the ruse.

But she appeared unfazed. "Isn't it still where you left it? You know we never disturb your carrel unless somebody specifically asks for the material."

Where I left it? My carrel? The material? What was she talking about? Of course I couldn't ask.

I muttered a confused "Thank you" and sidled away. I knew what a carrel was from my college days, but, as I glanced around the large room, I certainly didn't spot one here. Maybe if I just walked around, I'd get lucky and accidentally stumble across the right place.

With nothing to lose, I ambled back toward the stacks. I felt conspicuous, exposed. But as far as I could tell, no one was paying me the least bit of attention. I spotted a directory posted to the wall on my left. Glancing down the listings, the expected entries offered little hope—Autobiography, Biography, Circulation, an alphabetical parade of library services. All the locations were designated either 1, 2, or B. B is for basement? It seemed as good a place as any for hideaway carrels. With apologies to Sue Grafton, I went in search of a stairway.

I found the stairwell in the conjunction of the T, edged my way down the steps, and entered a rabbit's warren of tightly cramped bookcases.

"Hi, Derek." A young man with thick horn-rimmed glasses called to me from behind a desk piled with old magazines. I walked over to where he sat.

I gave him my safety-patented response. "Good morning."

"Haven't seen you around in a couple of weeks." He uttered the words as a statement, but his inflection appended a question mark.

"Been busy writing," I responded.

The man nodded. "Sorry about the broken glass," he said. "One of the janitors got a little slaphappy with his broom."

He had just marginally shifted his head to the right when he spoke. I followed his direction and spotted a tiny glass-enclosed cubicle. A piece of cardboard had been taped across part of the door.

Derek's carrel. I squelched a cry of triumph, but obviously not quite soon enough. I suppose the man interpreted the sound as a moan of complaint.

"They'll replace the pane this afternoon. And don't worry. No one disturbed a thing."

I entered Derek's domain with a smug sense of accomplishment, closed the door behind me, and emitted a self-satisfied sigh. Success! I had traversed a potentially dangerous obstacle course in near-world-record time. I spotted the light switch next to the door facing, flipped it on, and watched the fluorescent bulb in the ceiling grudgingly come to life. The only furniture in the otherwise bare cubicle consisted of a desk and a chair.

I walked over to the plasticoated desk. Papers and magazines littered the far side of the desktop, while three reels of microfilm were stacked neatly beside the monitor reader on the near side. A shelf above the desk contained about a dozen hardcover books.

The desk held no drawers, so anything I hoped to find had to lie in plain sight. I first checked through the books to see whether Derek's diary hid among them. Not really expecting to find it, I was not overly disappointed when it failed to appear.

I leafed quickly among the magazines and papers hoping to discover any handwritten notes Derek might have made. There were none. Had he made any notations, he clearly had not left them here. Lowell must have been right when he said Derek kept everything in his diary.

Sighing at my failure to blaze a shortcut through the material, I picked up one of the microfilm boxes. A label on its side identified it as the *Louisville Courier*—1954. The other two reels covered the years 1955 and 1956. Less than eager to attempt the scanning of three years of daily newspapers— especially since I didn't have the least idea of what I would be looking for—I shifted my attention instead to the books on the overhead shelf.

The titles did not offer any quick fix to my dilemma. *Corporate America, Private Company versus Public Corporation,* and *Giving Good Business* were representative of the selections. The one odd book that broke the thematic pattern was *Mountain Myths, Medicine and Magic* by some woman named Fern Woodgully. What a hoot!

It would take me days to read through all these books, and if my experience with doctrinaire texts held true, I'd be bored out of my skull. Even assuming that they contained information relevant to Derek's research on the Holcomb Company, I was fairly certain the only thing I would get out of them would be eyestrain. No, my best hope, and the reason I had left them for the last, resided in the magazines and papers. Especially the papers.

The papers were all photocopies of magazine and newspaper articles. Realizing that Derek had most likely made the copies and that he surely would have taken the most informative ones away with him, I held little optimism that I would turn up anything startling. I was wrong.

The first photocopy was from an October 1989 *Louisville Courier* article detailing Lindsey Brevard's succession to the presidency of the Holcomb Company following her father Lawrence's sudden retirement. The newspaper reporter intimated that Lawrence Brevard had not willingly stepped aside. A grainy black-and-white photo of Lindsey Brevard accompanied the article. Her age had been given as thirty-seven. I did a quick calculation, adding the intervening years, and realized that she now would be just slightly my senior.

The next sheet of paper came from a *Fortune* article printed last year that highlighted the company's assets—Lowell had indeed been correct with his seven-billion-dollar figure. The story elaborated the details of the Holcomb Company holdings, including paper, pharmaceutical, cosmetics, mercantile, and communications subsidiaries. The bottom line delineated a vibrant organization with an impressive profit margin.

Next up was an article from February of this year, taken from *People* magazine. It featured a brief profile of Lindsey Brevard, citing her as one of the nation's most powerful women business executives. It highlighted her years as head of the Holcomb Company, and focused primarily on the introduction of her personal line of cosmetics—a line that currently provided the company with its largest revenue leader.

The last sheet of paper was a lopsided misprint. The copier had obviously malfunctioned, cutting off the source citation as well as smudging major portions of the story. The sheet appeared to be a middle page of a longer article. I read the discernible portions of the story with growing excitement.

The article focused on Lindsey Brevard's thwarted legal maneuvers to break her late uncle's will. The writer gave a brief historical background. In the 1920s, John Holcomb had inherited a small paper mill from his father and had turned it into a thriving enterprise, diversifying into a number of related areas. Then World War II had accelerated the company's growth, and the postwar demand for its products— primarily paper and lumber—had catapulted the company into empire status.

Then, on Thanksgiving Day 1954, at the height of his success, John Holcomb had died in a tragic and mysterious accident in Lake Cumberland—an accident that had also claimed the lives of his wife and son. According to the writer, the only surviving member of his immediate family had been his sixteen-year-old daughter, Elizabeth, who had been too "indisposed" to attend the holiday outing.

John Holcomb's will left a seventy percent share in the company—he had also assigned the remaining thirty percent to his brother-in-law Lawrence Brevard—to his daughter Elizabeth, the same Elizabeth Holcomb who for the past four decades has been a voluntary resident at the Lansdale Sanitarium for the Mentally Ill.

The article then quoted Lindsey Brevard. "I'm sure Uncle

John never intended to stymie our growth. But until we can take the Holcomb Company public, we will never realize our full potential."

The author of the piece explained that since Elizabeth Holcomb had been a minor at the time her father had drawn up the will, he had included language that would retain her share in the company in an irrevocable trust until she reached maturity. Since John Holcomb had not specified a corresponding age for that maturity, the trustee of the estate—the Commonwealth National Bank—had steadfastly refused to turn over control of the company to an "emotionally unstable legatee." Lawyer jargon, I thought. The bank allowed the company's board, first under the direction of Lawrence Brevard and later his daughter Lindsey Brevard, to run the Holcomb Company. There was just one hitch—as long as Elizabeth Holcomb remained alive, the Holcomb Company stayed in private hands. However, were it to go public, estimates of its first offerings of common and preferred stock exceeded two billion dollars. The page ended in mid-sentence discussing Lindsey Brevard's next legal stratagem. I let the sheet of paper fall gently down to the desktop.

Wow, talk about a motive for murder!

What had Derek said that evening at the house, the only time I ever saw him alive—"I've got lots to say and, believe me, lots Kyle needs to hear." Talk to me now, Derek. Was this what you wanted to tell me? I know I'm making a huge and totally unsupported leap, and I also know that there are still a lot of gaps to be filled in. But I also know that you, in your investigative manner, progressed step by methodical step, checking and double-checking until you were satisfied, and

I'm guessing that you eventually reached the same point. And since I do know where you ended up—on my doorstep claiming me as your twin brother—can I prematurely fill in the blanks and reach the same conclusion? I ended my imaginary conversation with my dead brother, then reflected on my certain conviction.

Thanksgiving Day 1954. On the day John Holcomb died, his sixteen-year-old daughter had been "indisposed." I'd have to verify the dates, but regardless of the specific interval, there was no way Thanksgiving Day 1954 could fail to fall more than two weeks from another date with which I was intimately familiar—November 15, 1954.

The date on my birth certificate.

CHAPTER 11

"This author
prefers gentility
to grim reality, a spot
of tea
to a belt of whiskey,
a two-step instead of an
alley fight."

—Stokes Moran,

on Charlotte MacLeod's *The Recycled Citizen*

"Derek would have told me!"

"You said yourself that you had missed each other's phone calls. Isn't it possible that by the time you finally spoke to him, he was so preoccupied with finding me that he didn't mention anything else?"

Lowell shook his head emphatically. "I can't believe it. If Derek had suspected that Elizabeth Holcomb was his mother, he would have said something to me, I know he would have."

"How about this as an explanation? Derek didn't want to mention anything to you until he was sure, until he had proof."

Lowell frowned, but did not disagree. "What kind of proof?"

"I don't know," I said, then lunged at the first possibility that entered my head. "Maybe he was waiting for an eyewitness."

"An eyewitness?"

"Yeah. You know, someone who was around back then, who knew the family, who—hell, I don't know—somebody who knew something, anything."

Lowell nodded. "That makes sense. Derek was always very careful, always very cautious. Not like some people I could name." He cast me a sideways glance. "Derek consistently insisted on at least two sources before he would ever report a story."

Lowell paused for a moment, then came to a decision. "Okay, I can accept that explanation."

I smiled. With absolutely nothing concrete to go on except my wild imagination, my theory had passed its first crucial test—I had convinced Lowell it was possible. Not that he believed it, not even that he felt it was probable. Just that it was possible. If I had been an Olympic runner, I'd have earned a victory lap.

Obviously, my excitement over what I had discovered had made it impossible for me to patiently read through the remaining material in Derek's carrel. But I did take a few precious minutes comparing the typeface of the smudged photocopy with the various typefaces of the magazines on Derek's desk. I wanted desperately to locate the article from which the page had come, convinced that there would be other information in the report that potentially would be just as electrifying as what I'd already encountered. As I thumbed breathlessly through the magazines, I hoped against hope that, if at no other time in my life, then at this one moment luck would be with me. Finally, near the bottom of the stack, the *Kentucky Business Journal* matched. I hurriedly scanned down the periodical's table of contents and located a story entitled "Who's Minding the Holcomb Store?" Thank you, God, I silently prayed.

With a brain too fevered for common sense, I had unbuttoned my shirt, slipped the magazine into the waistband of my jeans, adjusted my clothing so that the bulge wouldn't show, and nervously walked out of the library. This was only the second time in my life I had ever stolen anything,* and I made a solemn vow that not only would I return the magazine to the library as soon as possible but I would also make a sizable donation to the Louisville Free Public Library in Derek's name. Anything to assuage the guilty exhilaration I experienced as I emerged through the library's front doors still a free man.

Once I had returned to the loft, while waiting for Lowell to get back from the mortuary, I read the article in its entirety. Somewhat disappointedly, I discovered that the meat of the story had been contained in the smudged photocopy. But with one exception—one very important exception as I saw it.

Near the end of the article, the reporter—whose byline identified her as business editor Marianne Clements—had violated standard journalistic practice to the extent that she had included an unsubstantiated rumor. Admitting that the story could not be confirmed, Clements had stated that Elizabeth Holcomb had recently been diagnosed with terminal cancer. But if true, the writer had claimed, then Lindsey Brevard's

*See *Otherwise Known as Murder* (Scribners, 1994).

ongoing battle to break the John Holcomb will would soon be moot. I had just closed the magazine when Lowell arrived.

He had big news too. Not as big as I thought mine was, but noteworthy nonetheless.

Lowell had finally explained his mysterious errands. While I was busy at the library, Lowell had dropped by Derek's bank to see if he could get a copy of Derek's most recent credit card transactions. Since one of the bank's vice presidents was Lowell's boyhood friend, Lowell had walked out fifteen minutes later with the last six weeks of Derek's credit card charges. Then, not satisfied with one coup, Lowell had strolled down the street to the phone company and asked for an up-to-the-minute accounting of all the toll calls made both to and from his telephone number. Thanks to Lowell's initiative, we now had the means to reconstruct some of Derek's movements and activities in the days leading up to his death.

"Well done," I had complimented him, admiring his ingenuity.

Now, sitting across from me at the kitchen table, Lowell industriously sorted through the varied documentation while I continued to interrupt him with my theories.

"We need to know exactly what was in John Holcomb's will," I said. "It might give us some clue as to the killer's identity."

Lowell looked up from his reading. "You don't seriously believe that had anything to do with Derek's death, do you?"

"Yes, I do. We're talking about big business and huge sums of money. You don't think anybody would let a little thing like murder stand in the way of a couple of billion dollars, do you?"

Lowell laughed disarmingly. "Not when you put it that way."

"But how can we get our hands on a copy of that will? Do you have any ideas?"

Lowell impatiently shuffled through the papers on the table. "I'll give a lawyer friend of mine a call if you will promise to be quiet so I can concentrate on what I'm doing."

"I promise," I said, then added with a grin, "if you'll call now."

Lowell uttered a frustrated but friendly grunt and picked up the telephone. I listened intently to his abbreviated side of the conversation. He quickly dispatched the usual preliminaries and moved straight to the point.

"Look, Jim, the reason I'm calling. I have a favor to ask. Yes. I'd like to know the contents of the John Holcomb will. Can you help me on that?"

Suddenly, Lowell's eyes locked rigidly on mine. A crease furrowed his forehead.

"I see," he said after a moment's pause. "No, Derek's . . . away."

"What is it?" I whispered urgently. "Tell me what's going on?"

Lowell waved me to silence. "Yes, I've got it. Will you? I'd really appreciate it. Thank you very much. Keep in touch. Bye."

He broke the connection and placed the telephone softly on the tabletop.

"Well?" I demanded.

"Jim thought it was strange." Lowell looked at me with zombielike eyes. "He said Derek had made the very same request just a couple of weeks ago. He then said why didn't I just ask Derek?"

Inanely, the first words to erupt inside my brain recalled the Agatha Christie novel under its British title, *Why Didn't They Ask Evans?* In Dame Agatha's story, the question had merely been an overlooked possibility. But in ours, it was too late. We couldn't ask Derek.

"What did he say?"

"He's sending me a copy of the will. He just happened to make an extra copy when he furnished Derek with one." Lowell's voice sounded hollow, and he answered without inflection.

"Did he give you any information from the will?"

"He told me the one thing he said Derek had been most interested in."

"What's that?" I demanded urgently, almost without breathing.

Lowell smiled. "Jim said when Elizabeth Holcomb dies, all her shares go to Lawrence Brevard, or his heirs. That is, unless—" Lowell paused.

"Unless what?" I could almost hear the arrhythmic beating of my heart.

"Unless she had a child," Lowell finally answered. "In which case, the child would inherit. Everything."

Bingo!

"You must realize, don't you, that if you're right about all this, then you stand to inherit a billion-dollar fortune?"

I had been so caught up in Derek's identity, in finding Derek's killer, that, in my mind, I had only been aware of Derek's position. But Lowell was right. Everything that had applied to Derek now also applied to me.

"I can't think of that right now," I said. "We've got more important matters to deal with."

"Oh my God!" Lowell suddenly exclaimed, jumping up from his chair and running toward the sofa.

"What is it?" I called, alarmed.

Lowell returned with a red parka in tow.

"It's Weezer," he said, unzipping one of the garment's compartments. "I forgot all about her."

"You had her in there?"

"I told you I take her with me everywhere."

Lowell lifted the sleepy animal from her cloth prison. With her eyes aslant, squinting against the light, she yawned, then stretched. Lowell held her lovingly against his cheek.

"Poor Weezer. I didn't mean to leave you in there so long. You must be starving."

He placed the little animal on the floor, and we both watched as she once again performed her stretch-and-yawn routine. Next, Weezer sniffed Lowell's shoes, then mine. Finally, she padded purposefully over to her food dish and began to eat.

"What does she eat?" I asked, enthralled. She really was a beguiling creature.

"Cat food. But not the fish flavor. She can't stand that. It has to be the meat, chicken, and milk combination."

I turned my attention away from the ferret, now munching loudly over her bowl. Lowell resumed checking through the phone records.

"There are several numbers here I don't recognize," he said. "And I know I didn't make the calls."

"Does it give their location?"

"Yeah. One is in New Albany, Indiana, and that same number has two listings. Once on May 4, and then again on May 6."

"Where's New Albany?" I asked, revealing my complete ignorance of local geography.

"It's just across the river."

"How long did those two calls last?"

"The first call took only four minutes, but the second call ran for thirty-eight minutes." He looked up. "Do you think that's significant?"

I nodded. "It could be. Thirty-eight minutes makes it more than just a wrong number. It means Derek was definitely interested. But in what?"

"Should I call the number, then, and find out whose it is?"

I shook my head. "I wouldn't just yet. What about the other numbers you didn't recognize."

"One's in Cumberland, Kentucky—"

I interrupted. "Cumberland. Is that anywhere near Lake Cumberland?"

"Yeah. How did you know?"

I smiled. "That's where John Holcomb and his family were killed."

"But that was over forty years ago."

"That doesn't mean there aren't still people around who may have witnessed the event."

Lowell's jaw dropped. "Derek's eyewitness."

"Exactly."

Almost like an electric shock, a disturbing possibility suddenly occurred to me. "I wonder?"

"Wonder what?"

I shook my head. "No"—I dismissed the idea—"it's too far-fetched."

"What?"

"I was just thinking what if the accident that killed John Holcomb and his family turned out not to have been an accident after all."

"What are you saying?"

I paused a minute before answering. "Just suppose Derek wasn't the murderer's first victim. But possibly the fourth."

CHAPTER 12

"But more than any character,
coming to terms
with the past
is
our hero's
biggest challenge."

—Stokes Moran, on James W. Hall's
Under Cover of Daylight

"Are you hungry?" Lowell's question suddenly reminded me that it was well past noon.

"What do you have in mind?" I asked.

"Well, I'm not much of a cook, but I'm great at punching numbers into the microwave."

I laughed. "You sound like me."

Lowell walked over to the refrigerator and opened the freezer compartment. "Let's see. We've got spaghetti and meatballs, chicken Alfredo, beef pot pie—"

I interrupted the litany. "Spaghetti and meatballs will do just fine."

"Great. We've got two of those, so we can both have the same thing."

Lowell pulled the processed entrées out of the freezer, ripped apart the containers, and punched holes in their plastic coverings with a fork. Then he placed each on a paper plate, set them both inside the microwave's belly, closed the door, and programmed the timer.

"See, I told you I was great with numbers," he said with a smile.

"I usually have garlic bread with my spaghetti," I suggested.

Lowell's smile brightened. "Great. I just bought a fresh loaf of bread. Why don't you take care of that while I make some iced tea?"

Me and my big mouth. I joined Lowell at the counter, opened the loaf of white bread I found there, and pulled out four slices. "What do I put them on?"

"How about some aluminum foil?" Lowell reached into a cupboard and produced a roll of Reynolds Wrap. He handed it to me, and I tore off a fifteen-inch section.

The refrigerator offered up the Squeeze Parkay, and I lavished it on the bread. "Where's the garlic?"

"On the shelf above you. Behind the Quaker Oats," Lowell directed. "But it's garlic salt. I hope you don't mind."

I didn't. It was all the same to me, and I liberally dosed the aromatic crystals on top of the margarine, then took a knife and spread the mixture evenly over the bread slices. Pleased with my handiwork, I opened the hinged door of the toaster oven, rotated the dial to the four-hundred-and-fifty-degree setting, and carefully placed the buttered bread underneath the coils. Then I closed the oven door and hit the ON button.

"Should be ready in a couple of minutes," I said with a flourish of accomplishment.

"Wonderful." Lowell was ladling ice cubes into a pitcherful of brownish liquid.

"Instant," I muttered without enthusiasm.

Lowell frowned. "I can steep some up for you, if you don't mind waiting."

"No, no. Instant is fine."

"Are you sure? It's no trouble."

"On second thought, I think I'll just have water."

My wife would have been the first to claim that two men alone together in the same kitchen would be a surefire recipe for culinary disaster, especially if I was one of the men. But I'm happy to report that the meal came off without a hitch, as long as you don't count the blackened and overly salted garlic bread, or the crispy pasta and spongy meatballs. Other than that, everything was fine.

After lunch, Lowell and I got back to the business of solving Derek's murder.

"I think it's time we interviewed the suspects," I said.

"What suspects?"

"Well, to start with, how about Lindsey Brevard?"

The ornate Holcomb Building occupied a full city block in downtown Louisville and provided weekday working space to more than a thousand employees, but Lindsey Brevard was not one of them. She held court instead at the ultramodern Brevard Cosmetics factory, which was located on the extreme outskirts of the city. Located so far, in fact, from the loft that it was a toll call just to ring her office.

Or so Lowell eagerly informed me after he matched the number the Holcomb Company receptionist had given me to one of the numbers from Derek's phone record.

"Now we're getting somewhere." His grin was contagious. I smiled back as I picked up the phone and dialed.

Grumbling but acquiescent, Lindsey Brevard's secretary penciled me in for a five o'clock appointment that very afternoon. But, she cautioned me, I might have to wait.

At 5:45 P.M., I was still waiting, cooling my heels in her outer office, when Lindsey Brevard finally opened the door to her inner sanctum and peremptorily beckoned me inside.

I entered her office expecting to find her regally entrenched behind a desk. Instead, she had taken a seat on a sofa in front of a plate-glass window that opened onto an enclosed patio. She leaned back against the cushions and casually crossed her sleek legs, showing them off to their best advantage.

"Have you finished the profile?" she asked as I settled into an overstuffed chair directly across from her.

Wing it, Derek, I thought. "Not quite," I answered.

"I thought that's why you wanted to see me," she said irritably. "I hope you know your deadline is little more than a week away."

I leaned toward her. "Don't worry. You'll get it." So I lied. Sue me. Someone else could break the bad news to Lindsey Brevard that that was one article she'd never see.

She gave me a cold half-smile. "I'd better." I could read the frosty warning in her words.

I didn't particularly like Lindsey Brevard. She was self-consciously attractive, arrogantly self-assured, and intentionally provocative. She was also one of the most powerful women in American business, successfully heading a billion-dollar company, a position that inherently requires toughness and ruthlessness, characteristics I was certain Lindsey Brevard possessed in ample measure.

"So why did you insist on this meeting?" She tossed her red hair in an affected manner.

"I just wanted a little additional information."

She extended her hands toward me, palms up. "What more could you possibly need? After our last interview, you already know everything there is to know."

I laughed nervously. "I doubt that."

"Okay, fire away." She stretched both arms out on the top edge of the sofa. Indicating what? An open book? Or an invitation?

I tried to come up with a question that Derek wouldn't have asked. "When was the last time you saw Elizabeth Holcomb?"

The question seemed to amuse her. "Why in the world do you want to know that?"

"I just wasn't clear on the nature of your relationship."

"There is no relationship. Elizabeth Holcomb is as crazy as a bedbug, and she's right where she belongs. And don't you dare quote me on that!"

"Excuse me." A tall silver-haired man stood framed by the doorway. "Lindsey, may I interrupt?"

"Yes, of course, come on in," she answered without turning around, her back to the man.

"Hello again." He nodded toward me.

"You remember Derek Winslow, don't you, darling? He's writing the profile on me for the annual report."

I inferred from her words that this mild-mannered man must be Daniel Whiting, Lindsey Brevard's long-suffering husband. According to one of the library articles, he was the chemical genius behind the successful Brevard cosmetics line.

"I'm sorry to intrude, dear," he said timidly, "but I needed your approval to accept this shipment." He proffered her a receipt. She took it, as well as the pen he supplied, and slashed her signature across the paper.

"Thanks," he said, backing out of the room.

"Controlled substances," she explained, possibly in answer to my unasked question. "I'm the only one authorized to accept delivery."

"I see. Now, getting back—"

From outside the room, I heard Daniel Whiting exclaim, "Oops! Sorry." Then another male voice, obviously younger and clearly angry, responded, "Can't you watch where you're going, you old fart!" A second later, an intense young man, hurriedly rearranging the papers in his hands, bolted into the room.

"Lindsey, I need—" When he looked up from his papers and saw me sitting there, he stopped his words in mid-sentence. "Derek! What are you doing here?"

"Mr. Winslow had some more questions to ask me." Lindsey Brevard answered for me. "You remember my assistant, don't you, Mr. Winslow? Philip Perdieu." I interpreted the belated introduction as a stab at sarcasm on Ms. Brevard's part. But her assistant took her words literally.

"Of course he remembers me," Philip Perdieu said snappishly. "Derek, you know you're supposed to channel all requests through me. Lindsey, I'm sorry about this. I'll provide Derek with whatever information he requires." Then, turning toward me, he demanded, "Come on, Derek, let's go."

"Mr. Winslow will be out in a minute," said Lindsey Brevard. "You can wait for him outside, Philip."

"But these papers—"

"Outside, I said."

Like a whipped puppy, Philip Perdieu turned on his heels and skulked from the room.

"You weren't very nice," I said.

"I'm the boss. I don't have to be nice. Now, where were we?"

"I was asking—"

"Oh yes. You were asking about Elizabeth Holcomb. Well, I don't want to talk about her. She has absolutely nothing whatsoever to do with this company. If that's what you came out here for, then you wasted both my time and yours." She stood up, a sign the interview was concluded.

I rose to my feet as well. As Kyle, I had a million more questions to ask. But as Derek, I was forced to swallow them.

"Thank you," I said lamely.

"For what?" With that, she closed the door behind me.

As directed, Philip Perdieu lay in wait for me just outside the door.

"Are you trying to get me fired?" he whispered furiously.

I really felt sympathy for the poor schmuck. "I'm sorry."

"You should be."

"It won't happen again," I promised.

"It better not. Not if you know what's good for you." With that, he turned and stalked off. I suddenly felt much less charitable toward the irksome Mr. Perdieu. Just who the hell was he, anyway?

"Is Mr. Lawrence Brevard in this building?" I asked the secretary who had been a forced witness to Perdieu's petulant tirade.

She gave me a quizzical look. "Mr. Brevard is retired, I thought you knew that."

"Yes, of course." I tried to cover my gaffe. "I was just told he was in the building today."

She misinterpreted my statement. "If Ms. Brevard says he's here, then he's here. You might try Mrs. Ketchum's office."

I followed the secretary's directions, walked down a long hallway, turned left, climbed three risers, turned right, and spotted the name Delores Ketchum on the wall outside her doorway. I knocked.

"Come in," a very feminine voice called.

I entered the office and waited. I had no idea whether Derek Winslow was known to Mrs. Ketchum. If so, it would be suspicious if I identified myself. I was hoping she would give me some signal of how to proceed. She did.

"Yes?" she said. "Do I know you?"

Thank you, God, I murmured. I would not have to watch what I said. It was obvious Derek had not been here before me.

"Excuse me?" She must have heard my heaven-sent gratitude.

"I'm Derek Winslow."

"Mr. Winslow, I was wondering when you'd get around to me," she said with a twinkle in her eye. I judged Delores Ketchum to be near sixty. She seemed dwarfed by the huge desk, the top of which was littered with papers and manuals of some kind. Her auburn hair was tinged with gray.

"I was told Lawrence Brevard might be here.'

She laughed, a warm and inviting sound. "Not likely." She glanced out her office window at the quickening twilight. "Right about now I'd guess Larry's doubling it up at the nineteenth hole."

"Can you tell me where I can find him?"

She eyed me suspiciously. "What do you want with Larry? I thought you were working on a story about dear little Lindsey." If her sarcasm was any indication, I'd say there was no love lost between Delores and her present employer.

"I wanted to talk to him about his late brother-in-law." Well, they always say honesty is the best policy.

"John Holcomb has been dead for forty years. What interest could you possibly have in him?"

I roosted gingerly on the edge of the visitor's chair. "Did you know him?"

"Of course I knew him," she answered sharply. Then, her tone softer, she asked, "What did you want to know?"

"Oh, I just needed some background information to flesh out my article."

Delores smiled at me. "I don't believe you. What is it you're really after?"

I hesitated. Fold or call? "I want to know how he died."

"Ha." It was a statement more than a laugh. But she did not elaborate further.

"Will Lawrence Brevard talk to me?"

"I doubt it." She paused, then leaned across the cluttered desk. "Tell me why you want to know," she insisted intensely, riveting her eyes into mine.

"It just seems"—I groped for the words—"that his death was a little bit too convenient."

Her gaze wavered, only a flicker and so slight I might have imagined it. But I hadn't.

"That's ridiculous," she answered, and leaned back in her chair. "And if I were you, I'd be careful about spreading slanderous rumors."

I stood up. "I'm sorry," I said. "I didn't mean to suggest—"

"Yes, you did." Her smile returned. "I'll tell Larry you were asking for him." I recognized it as the dismissal it was.

"Well, thank you anyway," I said, and headed toward the door.

"Mr. Winslow?"

I stopped and turned. "Yes?"

"Take care." I had never before heard those two innocuous words uttered more ominously.

"At least you made some progress?"

"You think so?"

Lowell nodded. "They now know that Derek Winslow is still around. That's one thing you definitely accomplished. Plus, you also met one of the principals. If your theory is correct, no one would gain more from Derek's death than Lindsey Brevard."

"But she's only in her mid-forties. She couldn't have had anything to do with John Holcomb's death."

"You never heard of a five-year-old murderer?" Lowell laughed.

"I don't think so." I laughed with him. "But her husband's

a possibility. He looked to be a good ten to fifteen years older than his wife."

"Did he seem the type?"

"The only killer profile Daniel Whiting would ever fit would be as the least likely suspect."

"Stranger things have been known to happen."

I leaned back against the sofa cushions. I was exhausted. It had been a long and arduous day, but it was not yet over. I still had to clear my confused and muddled thoughts.

"I'd really like to get a chance to talk with Lawrence Brevard," I said after a minute's reflection. "He seems to be the most obvious suspect in John Holcomb's death, but with his ouster at the company I can't see him still having a plausible reason to kill Derek."

"I agree," chorused Lowell. "I still think Lindsey Brevard is the only one who currently benefits from Derek's murder."

"I wonder how Delores Ketchum fits in," I said half aloud, ignoring Lowell's comment. "She's certainly nobody's fool."

"Well, you're definitely expanding our list of suspects."

"Yeah, but what I need to be doing is narrowing the list, not expanding it. And there's still so much we don't know."

"Why don't you sleep on it?"

That sounded like pretty good advice to me, so I took it.

CHAPTER 13

"The author
wins the reader's sympathy
with a warm
and loving approach
that is
no less persuasive
than a sledgehammer."

—Stokes Moran,

on Susan Conant's *Bloodlines*

$\mathcal{T}$he ferret woke me up.

Even in my half-consciousness, I sensed the little animal's presence under the bedcovers. But when she touched her cold nose against the sensitive skin of my abdomen, I came fully alert.

The morning sun streamed through the giant windows. Yawning, I stretched the life back into my muscles. Sleeping on the sofa had fast lost its charm, if it ever had any. I checked my watch and saw that it was 7:58. The ferret was better than an alarm clock.

I abandoned Weezer to her new nest, wrapped Derek's robe around my body, and padded barefoot over to the telephone. By the time I heard Lee's "Hello" on the other end of the line, it was precisely 8 A.M.

Half an hour later, after informing my wife of every little detail of my Louisville adventure, including my suspicion that Elizabeth Holcomb was my biological mother, I broke the connection and fled in desperation to the bathroom. With one urgent errand completed, I turned my attention to the next—morning coffee.

I had just poured the steaming liquid into my cup when Lowell climbed down the ladder from his nocturnal hideaway. He mumbled "Good morning," but neither of us was even marginally coherent until the caffeine kicked in, and in Lowell's case the nicotine as well.

"I've only seen you smoke a couple of cigarettes in the entire time I've been here. What kind of habit do you call that?"

He exhaled a rising pillar of smoke. "A bad one." We both laughed.

"Are you trying to quit?"

"Not so you could tell it, that's for sure." Lowell took another deep drag. "I only smoke about a pack a week. I can even go several days at a time without one."

"I've never heard of anything like it," I admitted, and proceeded to tell him about the tough time I'd experienced in kicking the habit. "Not a day, not an hour, goes by that I don't crave a cigarette. I even want one right now. Desperately."

He extended me his pack. "Oh no"—I waved it off—"my wife would kill me."

"Suit yourself." Lowell shrugged and returned the cigarettes to his shirt pocket. "What's on tap for today?"

"How far is it out to Lake Cumberland?"

The question seemed to surprise him. "It's about a hundred miles, I'd say. As the crow flies, that is. The lake is up in the eastern mountains, kind of in the middle of the state, and it would take at least three or four hours' driving time to get there."

"Why?" I asked, dumbfounded.

"Winding roads. Unpaved roads. Treacherous roads. Take your pick. Why do you want to go there?"

"I thought I might turn up something."

"After forty years?" Now it was Lowell who was dumbfounded.

"Yeah, I guess you're right." Another idea occurred to me. "Which of Derek's calls was made last?"

"Last?"

"Yeah. The most recent one?"

Lowell walked over to the kitchen counter and shuffled through the neat stack to which he had consigned them.

"It looks like the second call to New Albany is the latest. Why? What difference does it make?"

"Maybe none." I gestured for him to hand me the sheet. "But it's just possible that if Derek approached this like an empirical puzzle, then the later the call, the more relevant it might be."

"That's so confusing it sounds like something out of a detective novel."

"It is," I said, reaching for the phone and punching in the New Albany number.

"Hello." The voice on the other end of the line sounded like it belonged to an elderly lady.

"Yes." What do I say now? I finally opted for "Who's speaking, please?"

"This is Adelaide Crimm," she answered shakily, then with more vigor demanded, "Who's this?"

"This is Derek Winslow, Ms. Crimm."

There was no response. "Ms. Crimm? Are you still there?"

"Yes, Mr. Winslow, I'm still here." Her reply was almost wistful, maybe implying that at her age she was lucky to be anywhere.

"Ms. Crimm, I was wondering if I could come out to see you today?"

"Certainly, young man. Do you remember how to get here?"

"I think so," I lied. "But it might be a good idea if you refreshed my memory."

I motioned frantically to Lowell for a pencil, and I hurriedly scribbled the directions on a piece of paper Lowell had thoughtfully thrust under my hand.

"Thanks, Ms. Crimm," I said when she had finished her precise recital of street names and road turns. "I'll see you in a couple of hours?" I looked at my watch. "Let's say, around eleven?"

"That will be fine," she agreed meekly.

"Well?" Lowell asked as I placed the receiver down on the tabletop.

"It seems I have an eleven o'clock appointment with a little old lady."

"A little old lady? What's she got to do with all this?"

"I don't know," I answered. "But I definitely intend to find out."

Adelaide Crimm lived on Larchmont Avenue in New Albany, a broad tree-lined thoroughfare with Victorian-style homes dotting both sides of the street. I identified the house number she had given me and pulled Derek's Mustang into the narrow driveway.

I climbed five steep front steps, gained the level footing of the wooden porch, and touched the doorbell. While I waited for my summons to be answered, I glanced at my watch: 10:58. Almost exactly on time.

After a minute, I rang the bell again. Another thirty seconds elapsed before I heard the lock being turned and the door opened.

"I'm sorry to keep you waiting so long," she said by way of introduction, "but I was down in the root cellar and unfortunately I don't move as fast as I once did."

I judged Adelaide Crimm to be somewhere on the other side of eighty. A tiny, fragile-looking woman, she displayed a beaming smile and an intense blue-eyed gaze that belied her advanced years.

"Won't you come in?" she asked politely, turning awkwardly as I crossed the threshold.

I followed her into the interior of the house. She did indeed move slowly, taking almost two steps for every one of mine. The measured pace reminded me of my college graduation procession.

The inside of the house was as Victorian as its exterior— high ceilings, dark walls, the pervasive smell of furniture polish. The room to which she led me—well, there was no other word for it but parlor. Four narrow windows were flanked by heavily brocaded curtains. A fireplace, appearing forlorn by neglect, was crowned with a mantelpiece. Two overstuffed horsehair sofas faced each other across a mahogany table. Adelaide Crimm nestled on one, barely denting the springs, while I perched uncomfortably on the other.

"Ms. Crimm—" I began.

"Now, none of that. I thought last time we had agreed you'd call me Addie."

Right. I had to remember Derek had already spoken with her.

"All right, Addie—"

"Excuse me," she interrupted again. "Would you like a cup of tea?"

"No, thank you." It was harder getting a word in edgewise with her than it was with my neighbor Nolan back in Tipton.

"I'm afraid," I barged ahead, pulling a pad and pencil from my pocket, "that I've misplaced the notes from our previous conversation. Would you mind going through it for me again?"

I glanced down at the blank sheet of paper, pencil poised at the ready. When she didn't immediately respond, I looked back up.

Addie was staring at me, a tear welling in the corner of her left eye. "Are you all right?" I asked worriedly.

"Oh yes, I'm fine," she said. The tear slipped from the edge of her eye and tracked down her cheek. "It's just you're so handsome."

"Well, thank you," I stammered. I guess little old ladies can get overly emotional at the slightest provocation. "Can we continue?" I asked when she had backhanded the tear into oblivion.

"Certainly." She flashed me an uncertain smile, her face taut. "You wanted me to repeat what I've already told you?"

"That's right."

"I hate living in the past. And it was all so long ago. Are you sure it's necessary?"

I nodded. "It really is."

"Well," she began her narrative, "like I told you, I was John Holcomb's housekeeper for the last fifteen years of his life. And, believe me, it was not an easy home in which to live.

"He was gone most of the time, off on one business trip after another. His wife, Louise, was a burden, bless her soul, always demanding that things be done just so. She had been constantly pampered as a child, you see, and she expected the same treatment as an adult. But her biggest problem was the drinking. She had a real hard time with the alcohol. Not a day went by that she wasn't totally drunk by noon. Maybe if her husband had spent more time with his wife, her life might have been different. But there's no way of ever knowing.

"And then there was the boy. Robert. Hell on wheels he was, almost from the first day I met him. He had a real mean streak in him, that one. After he got on up in his teenage years, his father had to bail him out of one fix after another. Him and me never got along, I can tell you that, and I'm usually a pushover for kids.

"The only joy in the whole family was little Liz." Addie hesitated, then smiled. "I was with her almost from the day she was born. Poor sweet thing."

Addie stopped. "Are you sure I need to go on?"

"Oh yes, please?"

She smiled teasingly. "But you're not writing down anything."

Damn! I had been so engrossed in her story that I had forgotten to maintain the cover of taking notes.

"Well"—I searched frantically for an explanation—"I remember most of the general background. What I really need are the specifics about John Holcomb's death." I smiled encouragement.

She frowned. "Like I told you before, I wasn't there. I was taking care of Elizabeth."

"And she was ill?"

"That's right. Elizabeth had always been a fragile child, and I'm afraid she was having another one of her spells."

"Her spells?"

"That's what we called it back then." Addie looked off into space. "It was a mental thing. Heaven knows, no child ever had more reason—" She abruptly stopped in mid-sentence. "Where are my manners?" she said after a moment's pause. "Here it is almost lunchtime. Let me get you a bite to eat." She rose unsteadily to her feet.

"No, please, that won't be necessary," I protested, rising to my feet as well.

She gave me a dismissive wave. "Nonsense, I'll just be a minute." She teetered from the room.

It was obvious Adelaide Crimm had a lot more to tell. The only problem was—could I get her to tell it?

• • •

Lowell and I spent the afternoon digesting and dissecting John Holcomb's last will and testament, which had arrived at the loft by special messenger while I was still visiting Adelaide Crimm.

Despite my best efforts, I had been unable to get Addie to share any more information. Every time I had attempted to steer the conversation back to the Holcomb past, Addie had successfully sidestepped the ploy.

"More mincemeat pie?" is how she had deflected one of my last questions.

I vigorously shook my head. "I couldn't eat another bite."

"Then how about some more coffee?"

Again, I declined, covering the top of the cup with my hand. "No, really. It was all delicious, but I am truly stuffed." I pushed my chair back from the dining-room table and stood up.

"Now, Addie—" I began.

"Gran?" The back door banged shut. "Gran, I'm home."

An attractive slim young woman whom I judged to be in her early twenties pirouetted through the swinging dining-room door.

"Oh, I'm sorry, Gran," she said, halting her forward momentum, "I didn't know you had company."

Addie smiled. "Becky, come in, dear. Mr. Winslow and I just finished lunch." She walked over to the young woman, reached up with one hand, and patted her cheek. "I'm so glad to have you home. Are you hungry? Can I get you something to eat?"

"No, thanks, Gran, I picked up something on the road."

"Oh, where are my manners?" Addie flustered. "Mr. Winslow—"

"There's no need for introductions, Gran," Becky interrupted. "Mr. Winslow called me in Bloomington a couple of weeks ago." When Addie turned back toward me, Becky shook her head firmly, a clear signal for me to keep quiet. But about what?

"That's right, Addie," I covered as best I could, "we had a nice little chat, didn't we, Becky?"

The young woman frowned. Had I said too much?

"Then you know she's in her third year at the university," Addie bragged as the three of us walked slowly toward the front door. "She's smart as a pistol, but then you have to be for premed, don't you, Becky?" Addie slipped her arm around Becky's waist and squeezed. "And I get to have her home with me for the whole summer because she starts an apprenticeship program—"

"Gran," Becky interrupted, obviously uncomfortable with Addie's effusiveness, "you're embarrassing me."

"Nonsense," snapped Addie. "It's the truth."

The three of us had finally reached the front door. "Well, I must be going," I said. "Thank you for a wonderful meal, Addie."

"Anytime, young man," she said, then added with a wink, "I enjoy the male company."

"I'll just see Mr. Winslow out to his car, Gran," Becky said. "Be right back."

We both stepped out onto the porch, and Becky closed the door behind us. She then expelled a huge breath.

"Thank you for not giving me away," she said.

Sure, no problem. What the hell was she talking about? I had no other option but to play along.

"Sure, no problem," I said.

"You see, I ditched class that day," Becky explained almost offhandedly, "and something like that always upsets Gran."

Ditched class? Why would she ditch class to take one little phone call? There was obviously more to the story than that—but, dammit, I couldn't ask. There were times when being Derek Winslow sure had its drawbacks.

"I understand," I said, not understanding a blasted thing.

"You're a peach," she said, and turned to reenter the house. I couldn't just let her go, not without finding out what she and Derek had discussed. She apparently had something important to contribute; otherwise, why had Derek sought her out?

"Becky?" I called. She stopped and turned back toward me. "I seem to be having a little memory lapse. Maybe you could refresh—"

"Oh, you are a card." She kissed me full on the lips. "There, does that help?" she teased, then quickly disappeared behind the door.

I stood there momentarily stunned. Needless to say, I was now more confused than ever.

"Adelaide Crimm is definitely a suspect," Lowell said.

"Oh, come on, the woman's eighty if she's a day."

Lowell laughed. "I'm not talking about Derek's death. What I meant was that if John Holcomb and his family were indeed murdered, then Adelaide Crimm had as good a motive as anybody."

I disagreed. "As far as I'm concerned, Lawrence Brevard still gets that honor."

The terms of John Holcomb's will were basically as reported in the *Kentucky Business Journal*. But there were a couple of interesting points the article had failed to mention.

First, of course, was the Adelaide Crimm provision, which is what Lowell and I had just been discussing. She had been left an annual stipend of fifty thousand dollars for the rest of her life. Why? In 1954 terms, that seemed like an excessive amount of money to leave a housekeeper. Not to mention that over the course of the next forty years, she had collected a grand total of two million dollars. People surely have been murdered for a lot less. So granted, Addie did have a motive.

The second surprise had been the dating of the will. John Holcomb had signed it on November 20, 1954, just a matter of days prior to his death. Why? Was the timing significant? It would have been interesting to have seen how this last will had differed from its previous incarnation.

Concerning the disposition of the Holcomb Company, the will had specified four legatees. According to the terms of the document, seventy percent of the Holcomb Company was to be divided evenly among Elizabeth Holcomb, her mother, Louise, and her brother, Robert. But since Louise and Robert had both died at the same time as her father, Elizabeth got the whole seventy percent, except that her inheritance was to be held in an irrevocable trust until she reached maturity, a judgment left to the discretion of the will's trustee—the Commonwealth National Bank of Louisville. The same wording had applied to Robert Holcomb as well. So had she survived her husband, Louise Holcomb would have been in a position to exercise total control of the company, at least theoretically. Finally, and this was the clause that seemed most enigmatic, at the death of the last of the three legatees, the entire seventy percent would once again be shared equally by all remaining direct-line descendants, meaning grandchildren, perhaps even great-grandchildren, and so on. In other words, John Holcomb had made it impossible for any of the three legatees to retain more than a life interest in the company.

The fourth legatee had been the brother-in-law, Lawrence Brevard, who had been assigned the remaining thirty percent of the company outright, with no similar life restriction on his share.

Finally, John Holcomb ended the document with a bold threat. In common vernacular, he warned that should any of the beneficiaries be so foolhardy as to challenge the explicit terms of the will, and fail, they would forever forfeit their rights of inheritance.

"I still have a couple of questions," I said after going through the will a second time.

"Only a couple?"

I ignored Lowell's gibe. "Why did John Holcomb separate Lawrence Brevard from the others? And, for that matter, why did Lawrence Brevard get anything at all?"

"He was Holcomb's brother-in-law," said Lowell.

"Exactly. How many times are brothers-in-law ever mentioned in wills?"

Lowell shrugged. "Beats me."

"I wouldn't think too often."

"So what are you saying?"

"Just that John Holcomb must have had a powerful reason for leaving thirty percent of his company to Lawrence Brevard. Right now I'd give my eyeteeth to know what that reason was."

The telephone rang. Lowell picked it up, then handed it to me.

"Derek Winslow?" The voice was a deep baritone.

"Yes."

"This is Lawrence Brevard. I hear you've been looking for me."

"That's right."

"Bluegrass Cafe. Thirty minutes." The line went dead.

CHAPTER 14

*"The author
places his characters
in a harsh and unforgiving
world
where bad things
do indeed happen to
good people,
and where good people frequently
die."*

—Stokes Moran, on Robert Barnard's *Fête Fatale*

$\mathcal{L}$owell drove me to the Bluegrass Cafe.

After I had relayed to him the short gist of Lawrence Brevard's call, Lowell had suggested that, while I talked with Brevard, he could spend, say, half an hour at a haberdashery that was located in the same block as the cafe, then he could meet me back at the Bluegrass, where we could have dinner. I gratefully accepted the offer, since not only did I need help in locating the Bluegrass Cafe, I was also growing tired of Lowell's microwave cooking. Especially when he added that the Bluegrass had the best steaks in all Louisville.

Rain began to splatter against the windshield of Lowell's

BMW just as he maneuvered the pricey car into a vacant parking slot directly across the street from the trendy restaurant.

"Do you think it's safe to park on the street like this?" I asked skeptically.

"This is not New York, remember?" Lowell laughed. "Don't worry. The car will be fine."

"If you say so." I was still not convinced.

"Sorry, I didn't bring any umbrellas," he apologized. "Guess we'll have to run for it."

With the rain now pelting a loud symphony on the BMW's roof, Lowell and I bolted from the car, scampered across the street, and darted under the protective canopy covering the front entrance of the restaurant.

"Where's the men's store you mentioned?" I asked, shaking the water from my hair.

"Just about half a block." Lowell indicated the direction with his head.

"It wouldn't matter if it was right next door," I said. "Without an umbrella, you'll get soaked." The rain pounded the cloth overhang and bounced off the nearby pavement. I now had to shout to be heard. "Forget it. Just come inside with me."

The wind began to whip the spray up into our faces. Lowell nodded and followed.

"Whew," he said when the pressurized door finally closed behind us. "Talk about a downpour."

"Good afternoon, gentlemen." The hostess greeted us with a businesslike smile. "Table for two?"

"I'm meeting someone," I explained. "Mr. Lawrence Brevard?" Her smile brightened noticeably. "You must be Mr. Winslow?"

I nodded. "Mr. Brevard is already here," she said. "I'll take you to his table."

Lowell tugged the sleeve of my shirt. "I'll wait at the bar," he whispered.

I followed the hostess into the dark main cavern of the Bluegrass Cafe. She blazed a serpentine trail that eventually delivered me to a table where an elderly man sat nursing a drink. Observing our approach, he tilted back his head and drained the glass.

"Mr. Brevard? I'm Derek Winslow."

"I know who you are, boy. Don't be so formal. Sit down." He waved impatiently at the chair across from him, then gestured to a passing waiter that he needed a refill.

"Can I get you a drink?" Brevard asked me after I was seated.

"What are you having?"

"Good Kentucky bourbon."

"Club soda," I said. Brevard frowned, but he dutifully relayed my request to the waiter.

I judged Lawrence Brevard's age at seventy-five, give or take a year or two. Red spidering veins were visible on his face, and his hair—the little that remained, that is—was a washed-out white. Hard to tell, of course, with the table between us, but he did not give me the impression of being a tall man, and I estimated that he carried at least fifty more pounds than his height table recommended. Add in his pasty pallor, and I suspected he held an overdue notice on a coronary. It seemed to me that Lawrence Brevard was living on borrowed time.

"Now, what is it you want?" Brevard demanded after the waiter had delivered our drinks.

Deciding that catching him off guard was probably my only chance, I said bluntly, "For starters, I'd like to know why John Holcomb left you thirty percent of his company?"

He laughed, a hawking sound that quickly escalated into a rasping cough. To stop the spasm, he gulped his drink.

"You are a corker," he said, once he regained his voice. "What if I say it's none of your damn business."

"That won't end my questions."

"Who the hell do you think you are!" He slammed his fist down hard on the table, succeeding not only in startling me but also in rattling the silverware as well as capturing the attention of several nearby patrons.

"Mr. Brevard, I didn't mean—"

"Didn't mean what, my boy?" His voice was once again calm, his demeanor polite. Strangely, his burst of rage had disappeared as suddenly as it had come.

I opted for a different question. "Mr. Brevard, why did your daughter oust you from the company?"

He wagged his head from side to side. "There you go again," he said, but this time he retained his composure. "Lindsey did no such thing. It was time for me to step down, that's all."

"But you still retain your shares in the company, don't you? As far as I know, your daughter doesn't have any."

"Ah." He leaned back in his chair. "I see you don't understand the world of high finance." He signaled for another drink.

Brevard adopted a conspiratorial tone. "My boy, the board made the decision."

"The board?"

He nodded, deeper and deeper until his chin finally came

to rest against his chest. For a minute, I thought he had fallen asleep. Then his head jerked up, and he surged back into speech. "The board, the bank, what difference does it make? It's all the same thing."

"I don't understand," I admitted. The waiter placed another bourbon in front of Brevard.

"It's simple." He grinned, then downed half the fresh drink in one swallow. "The Holcomb Company is run by a board of directors. And the Commonwealth National Bank, as trustee for Elizabeth Holcomb, holds three of the four seats on the board. So it's simple," he repeated, "I was just outvoted. Or voted out's more like it." Brevard laughed at his own joke.

"I see."

He looked at his watch. "Lord, I've gotta get a move on." He reached inside his jacket—I assumed for his wallet—but instead he pulled out a plastic bottle. He unscrewed the cap, palmed a pill of some kind, and downed it with the last of his drink.

"Are you on medication?" I asked as he rose unsteadily to his feet.

"What?" He appeared momentarily confused, then his face cleared. "Oh, you mean this?" He held up the container. "No, no. These are just vitamins. Best thing our company ever made. They've changed the packaging over the years, but never the formula. My brother-in-law came up with that more than fifty years ago. Here, try one." He thrust the bottle into my hand.

"I don't know," I said hesitantly. I rolled one of the liquid gel caps out onto the tabletop.

"Well, suit yourself. Keep them with my compliments, anyway. And don't worry about the bill, that's taken care of."

With those final words, Lawrence Brevard left the table. I was hardly aware of his absence. Almost trancelike, I continued to stare at the vitamin.

At the means of Derek's death.

"Well, at least now we know why Derek suddenly started taking vitamins," Lowell said.

"Do we?" I asked absently.

Lowell, who had been watching from the bar, had joined me at the table shortly after Brevard's departure. Between the time the waiter had taken our order and the time the food had arrived at our table, I had been able to fill Lowell in on the details of my conversation with Lawrence Brevard.

"Sure," Lowell said, cutting a chunk from his porterhouse steak. "Those vitamins were a link to his family, to his grandfather. John Holcomb formulated those vitamins, so of course Derek would take them. It makes perfect sense to me, and, remember, I knew Derek better than anyone."

It made perfect sense to me too, and that was the problem. I had been so convinced that once we knew why Derek had suddenly started taking vitamins, we would be that much closer to identifying his killer. Now, I couldn't see how this information helped further the investigation at all.

"What's the matter?" asked Lowell, stuffing a forkful of rare beef into his mouth. "Don't you like your prime rib?"

"Oh, the food's great." I had only halfheartedly toyed with my steak; I couldn't even remember how it had tasted. For

Lowell's benefit, I dutifully picked up my knife and fork, sliced off a large piece of meat, and crammed it in my mouth. "See?"

Lowell laughed. "I've seen less pained expressions from men on death row. Now tell me what's really the matter."

So I did.

"I guess I just feel we're not getting anywhere," I concluded. "I don't know if I'm any closer to solving Derek's murder today than I was on the day he was first killed."

Lowell gently placed his knife and fork on the tabletop. "Then why don't we turn the whole thing over to the police and let them handle it?"

"I thought you wanted to find Derek's killer?"

"I do." Lowell reached across the table and tenderly touched my hand. "But if that's not going to happen, then I want to mourn him, and remember him, and bury him. And none of that is possible as long as we both keep pretending he's still alive."

I looked into Lowell's eyes and finally, fully, understood the pain he had intentionally kept hidden—from himself as well as from me. This man had been Derek's partner in love and in life for the past twelve years, and I had selfishly robbed him of the opportunity, the privilege, the right, to grieve.

I smiled and squeezed his hand in return. "Perhaps you're right. Perhaps it is time to let the experts take over."

"Good." Lowell picked up a French fry with his right thumb and forefinger, unzipped his parka with his left hand, and held the potato temptingly over the opening in the cloth. Almost immediately, a little pink snout furtively nosed through the opening and snagged the fry out of Lowell's hand, then just as abruptly disappeared back into the depths of the parka.

"Lowell!"

"Don't be so shocked," he said. "I had this parka specially made with a compartment just for Weezer."

"You'll get us kicked out of here," I whispered, glancing nervously over my shoulders. "Why risk feeding her French fries?"

"She doesn't like steak."

"That's not what I meant," I said irritably. "I wanted to know why."

Lowell laughed. "I guess she's a vegetarian."

I groaned. "I give up," I said, admitting defeat.

Lowell, apparently having mercy on me, finally offered a straight answer. "I told you," he said, "I take Weezer with me wherever I go."

Obviously, I concluded. Even to restaurants.

The rain had stopped by the time Lowell and I left the restaurant, and the clouds had been swept away by a freshening breeze. It was not even seven o'clock, yet the May twilight was so dark that the streetlights were already burning. The crescent-tipped new moon, incandescent against the evening sky, looked like the white edge of a woman's thumbnail, cut close to the skin.

I never saw the car. One second I was walking across the street, the next I was lying in the gutter, water gurgling under me. Eventually, I heard voices floating above me—

"You're going to be all right."

"The paramedics are on their way."

"Don't move."

"The police will be here any minute."

"Lie still."

My eyes felt encrusted in cement. Finally, I forced them open, struggling to clear my blurred vision. I looked down at my hands. They were cut and bleeding.

"No, you mustn't move." I turned my head painfully toward the man's voice.

"What happened?" I croaked.

This time a woman answered. "I saw the whole thing," she said, tucking a blanket around my shoulders. "A car came right at you. If your friend hadn't pushed you out of the way—"

"Lowell?" I struggled to sit up.

"You must stay down," she insisted. "We don't know how seriously you're hurt."

"Where's Lowell?"

"If you mean your friend, he's over there." I followed her gaze and saw a circle of people standing some ten yards away. "He wasn't quite so lucky," she said.

"Here, what are you doing?" It was the man's voice again.

What do you think I'm doing, you moron? I'm crawling. Or trying to, that is. At least it was reassuring to know that my elbows and knees were still working.

The woman said, "No, you can't do this." Who says I can't?

My two guardians moved along with me, but they did not attempt to impede my progress. Finally, after what seemed an eternity, I crawled through the circle of people around

Lowell. His body was crookedly sprawled on the asphalt. Blood pooled around his head, but I could see the rise and fall of his chest. He was alive.

I crawled to a point where my head was level with his. "Lowell?" I whispered. "Lowell, can you hear me? It's Kyle."

His eyelids flickered briefly, then opened. His voice barely audible, he said, "No more Derek, huh?"

I shook my head.

He grinned, then grimaced with pain.

"Weezer?" His tone was urgent.

Luckily, Lowell's parka had flared out from under him, and I didn't waste a second in getting it unzipped. I reached my hand down into the parka's depths and pulled out the squirming little animal, obviously frightened but—thank you, God—very much alive and kicking.

"Weezer's fine," I said, my voice breaking.

"Let me see her," he asked. I placed the ferret next to the right side of Lowell's face. She nuzzled his cheek and licked the inside of his ear. His left hand moved jerkily up to stroke her fur. He smiled.

"Take care of her for me, will you?"

I could feel the sting of tears behind my eyes. "Don't be silly," I said. "You'll be able to take care of her yourself."

But Lowell proved those words a lie. Less than a minute later he died, Weezer sleeping contentedly under his hand, the smile still fixed to his lips.

CHAPTER 15

"Of course,
the scenario would not be complete
without
the necessary dime-store
philosophy,
and you'll find it here
in abundance."

—Stokes Moran,

on Mike Lupica's *Dead Air*

$\mathcal{L}$ee walked down the passenger debarkation ramp at the Louisville International Airport the following morning, her overnight bag gripped tightly in one hand, a copy of *Good Housekeeping* held loosely in the other.

I had phoned her the previous evening from the hospital. The paramedics who had responded to the emergency call had insisted I get X rays, even though their cursory examination had revealed nothing more serious than a few lacerations and contusions.

The patrol cops had concurred. "You might have a concussion," one of the uniforms had advised, "or even a hairline fracture. It's best that you go ahead and find out."

So, after a brief preliminary interrogation, the police-men—with the redundant promise of more questions to come—had released me to the ambulance driver, who had rushed me, siren blasting, to Dumbarton Medical Center, where, after two hours of testing and prodding, the emergency room physician had declared that, with the exception of a few cuts and bruises, I was basically unhurt. So much for his advanced degree—the paramedics had outjargoned him.

So, after I had been medically vetted by the doctor, I had walked out into the reception area to find two plainclothes detectives waiting for me. I had immediately sensed it was going to be a long night.

"And after they let me call you," I informed my wife in the Mustang on the way back to Derek's loft, "Lieutenant Rick-etts and Sergeant Brent took me down to police headquar-ters, where they grilled me until three o'clock this morning." I looked at my watch. "Only four short hours ago," I calculated irritably. "So that should let you know how much sleep I managed to get."

What I failed to share with Lee was how skeptical the homicide detectives had initially been about my claim that I had been the driver's intended victim. In the beginning, they had approached the case as a standard hit-and-run accident. They even had well-meaning eyewitnesses who substantiated that interpretation. The one thing that had finally changed their minds, the one thing that had ultimately made the two detectives view the case as premeditated murder—as well as the one thing that had taken up most of the rest of the night—had been my telling them, albeit belatedly, about Derek's murder and my subsequent plan to catch his killer. I even gave them good old Pitkin as a reference. I had also asked them to keep the matter as confidential as possible.

"Both Derek Winslow and Lowell Dodge were well known here in Louisville," the one named Ricketts had said, "I don't know how long we can keep news like this out of the paper."

"Can't you delay even a day?" I had implored.

"Well," Ricketts had drawled, "I suppose we can tell the media we're not giving out the name of the victim until the next of kin has been notified."

"Great," I had said.

"But that only gets you twenty-four hours," he had warned.

I had nodded. Yeah, just twenty-four short hours in which to catch a killer.

"What happened to the ferret during all this?" Lee interrupted my thoughts.

I smiled. "The policemen and paramedics at the scene were kind enough to let me take Lowell's parka, and I kept Weezer close to me for the rest of the night."

"Even in the hospital?" The notion seemed to shock my wife.

I nodded. "I'm afraid, though, that I was not too gracious with some of the medical personnel, who had some Neanderthal ideas about animals not being allowed in the examination area. But Lowell saved my life, and I promised him that I would take care of Weezer, so I was not about to let her out of my sight. Not for a single minute."

"But that's not practical," Lee objected. "You can't take the ferret with you everywhere you go."

"Why not?" I asked, then added matter-of-factly, "Lowell did."

"That's ridiculous."

I grinned, unzipped the parka, and let her glimpse the slumbering animal. "Is it?"

Lee laughed and wagged her head. "You're something else," she admitted, gently stroking Weezer's fur. "You both are," she amended softly. "Well, I guess that means Bootsie has a new playmate."

"You can count on it," I promised.

"I've already told you. I never saw a thing."

Lieutenant Ricketts had knocked on the door of the loft just minutes after Lee and I had returned from the airport. While Lee unpacked, the lieutenant had resumed his questioning.

"So you don't know anything that could give us even a hint as to the identity of the driver?"

I shook my head sadly. "No. Nothing."

"As you suggested, I gave Sergeant Pitkin a call, and he basically verified everything you told us last night," Ricketts drawled. "Except that he did say he tried to discourage you from getting involved in the investigation yourself."

"Derek was my brother," I said. "I had to do something."

The night before, when I had finally spilled the whole story of Derek's murder to the two homicide detectives, neither had been particularly pleased that I had kept Derek's death a secret from the Louisville authorities.

"Amateurs have no place in criminal investigations," Ricketts had muttered then. Today he added, "It's best to leave the police work to the professionals." Each statement held the unspoken recrimination that, had I stayed out of the matter,

Lowell would still be alive. Well, nobody had to tell me that—
I knew it better than anyone.

After all, I had initially come to Louisville with the exalted
confidence that I alone could nab the killer, that I alone could
bait a trap that would prove impossible for the killer to resist.
Well, I had accomplished my objective, all right. As intended,
I had forced the killer's hand. But Lowell had paid the ulti-
mate price for my conceit. And even though my plan had
worked, I was still no closer to identifying the murderer. Talk
about tragic irony! All I had actually managed to accomplish
was to get an innocent person killed. At the moment, it looked
like the murderer had won.

"Pitkin is sending me everything he's got on the Winslow
murder," Ricketts said. "Including the autopsy report. Maybe
something in his material will help us in our investigation."

Yeah, right. I felt like telling him not to expect too much
from the inept Pitkin. But cops belong to a kind of brother-
hood where criticism of one translates into criticism of all. So
I kept my mouth shut.

Happily for me, Lieutenant Allan Ricketts demonstrated a
marked contrast to Tipton's finest. Professional in both demeanor and attitude, Ricketts displayed a self-confident assur-
ance that made it possible for me to believe he could indeed solve
the case. Older than other policemen I've encountered—I
judged him to be in his mid-fifties—Ricketts possessed a natural maturity that went even deeper than his years. While not
quite as rumpled as Columbo, as fat as Cannon, or as bald as
Kojak, he nevertheless came close to matching all three in
overall seediness. Still, I found I liked the man, but, more
importantly, I felt I could trust his quiet-spoken authority.

"I want you to let us handle everything from here on out," Ricketts warned. "There's no sense in asking for trouble."

"I agree," said Lee. Finished at last, I assumed, with her unpacking, my wife stepped off the bottom rung of the ladder and walked toward the sofa, where Ricketts and I had been holding our impromptu kaffeeklatsch.

I performed the requisite introductions. The lieutenant rose to his feet, nodded an acknowledgment to Lee, then added, "I want you to stay put, both of you. More than likely the killer will try to come after you again. I'm going to assign some men for your protection, but, even with that, I think the safest place for you is right here. Do I make myself clear?"

I nodded my understanding, but that didn't mean I necessarily agreed to his terms. Derek and Lowell were both dead, and I was now more determined than ever to find their killer.

"It was nice meeting you, ma'am," Ricketts said as he departed. "I'll keep in touch."

"Are you going to follow his wise advice?" Lee asked after Ricketts had gone.

I grinned sheepishly.

"I didn't think so," commented my wife.

"This place is something else," Lee said an hour later, after I had given her a step-by-step account of my stay in Louisville and followed that up with a walking tour of the loft. Now, standing in front of the floor-to-ceiling bank of windows, she gazed back into the interior of the loft. "All these gadgets and gizmos."

I couldn't interpret from my wife's tone whether her remarks indicated approval or disapproval. Which was okay, because I still wasn't sure of my opinion either. Like they say, it might be a nice place to visit, but I didn't think I'd ever want to live here. Not on any kind of permanent basis, that is.

"Where's the ferret?" Lee asked.

"Why are you so preoccupied with Weezer?"

She shrugged an explanation. "I'm not used to having her around. I'm afraid either I'll step on her or, what's even more scary, she'll step on me. And when I'm least expecting it too."

I laughed, remembering my first reaction to the furry little creature. "She's still in Lowell's parka," I confessed.

"Why are you keeping her hidden away in there? Won't she suffocate?"

"No. According to Lowell, she likes dark, enclosed spaces."

"But surely not all the time?"

I frowned. "I'm afraid if I let her loose, I'll never find her again. This is an awfully big room."

"I know, but she's got to have exercise, not to mention food, water, and fresh air." Lee walked over to the sofa, where I had earlier deposited Lowell's parka, unzipped the special compartment, and freed the ferret from her confinement. The little animal squinted against the sunlight, then hopped down off the sofa, and scurried over to her food dish.

"Is she housebroken?" Lee inquired.

"Yes, she uses a litter box, just like a cat."

"Where is it? I don't want to go stepping in it or knocking it over by accident."

"It's hidden away inside that cabinet." I nodded toward the counter next to Weezer's water bowl.

"It's closed," Lee protested. "How does she get to it?"

"Oh, Weezer's very resourceful. She opens the door."

"Now, that's something I've got to see."

The telephone rang. I picked it up.

"Mr. Malachi? This is Allan Ricketts. Sorry to bother you again so soon, but I thought you'd like to know. We just found the hit-and-run car."

CHAPTER 16

*"The main character
is a cynical
yet appealing hero
whose absurdities
merely
mirror society's own."*

—Stokes Moran,

on Robert Upton's *A Killing in Real Estate*

"Well, that was a big waste of time."

Following Lieutenant Ricketts' directions, Lee and I, with Weezer in tow, had driven to Poindexter Park, located on the outskirts of Louisville. We arrived in less than thirty minutes.

"The car was stolen," Ricketts had commented as we walked toward the dark blue Oldsmobile Ninety Eight. "Unfortunately, the only prints we've lifted so far belong just to the car's owner."

"Are you certain the vehicle was actually stolen?" I questioned. "Isn't it possible that the owner's just making that claim to avoid responsibility?"

Ricketts had laughed. "I wish it could have been that simple. But no, there's no chance of a false report."

"Why?"

"For several reasons. For one, the car was reported stolen at just about the same time as the accident, and for another, the owner filed the report in person at the Jefferson Street precinct, which is a dozen miles from the accident scene. And finally"—and here Ricketts had grinned broadly—"the owner of the automobile is Bishop William Knowles of the Louisville Catholic diocese."

Yeah, I'd say that just about eliminates the car's owner as a suspect. I walked around the big sedan, observed the crumpled front fender, the shattered windshield, and the mud-obscured license plate. I shuddered. It was quite an impressive murder weapon.

"You didn't turn up clues of any kind?"

Ricketts shook his head. "No. The engine was cold when the beat patrolmen discovered the car a couple of hours ago. We figure it was abandoned here sometime early last night. In fact, I suspect the killer brought it here directly after the accident."

Accident? Why did he persist in calling it an accident? It had been nothing less than cold-blooded murder. Just ask Lowell.

"Are you able to identify the vehicle at all?"

This time, I shook my head. "Like I told you before, I don't remember seeing a thing."

"Not even a blur?"

"I wish I could say yes. But I'm afraid I don't even remember Lowell pushing me out of the way. One second I was walking across the street, the next people were standing over me telling me to lie still. I'm sorry."

Ricketts sighed. "So am I."

"Did any of the eyewitnesses get a look at the driver?"

"Nothing that would stand up in court. One man thought the driver was a black teenage boy, another that it might have been an elderly Jewish woman. I think in each case the recollection was only personal prejudice coming to the fore."

I nodded. "What happened to Lowell's BMW?"

"I called his sister last night, and she came down and picked it up first thing this morning."

Sister? Lowell never mentioned he had a sister. Just as with Derek, there were so many things about Lowell I didn't know. And now would never have the opportunity to find out.

Lee, who had remained silent during this long interchange, suddenly spoke. "Have any funeral arrangements been made yet?"

Ricketts was slow to respond. "We haven't yet released the body to the family. I'm sure a funeral service will be scheduled fairly soon after the coroner is finished with the autopsy. But frankly, right now I couldn't even hazard a guess as to when that might be."

I had a sudden inspiration. "How do you think Lowell's family would feel about a joint memorial service for both Derek and Lowell?"

"I don't know," answered Ricketts. But Lee said more enthusiastically, "Kyle, I think that's a wonderful suggestion."

"Could you ask them?" I directed the request to Ricketts.

"Me?" The lieutenant seemed stunned by the notion. "Why me?"

"I'm a stranger," I explained. "I don't want to intrude on their grief." *Oh, that's real high-toned, Kyle. But why don't you tell the man your real reason? That you feel responsible for Lowell's death, and that you're too big a coward to face his family.*

"All right," Ricketts agreed, "I'll mention it to them." Why had he so quickly capitulated? Was it possible he could read my thoughts?

"What now?" Lee asked, once we had returned to the relative safety of the loft and spread six containers of Chinese takeout all across the kitchen table.

"What do you suggest?" I turned the question back on her.

"You know," she said, opening a paper carton of moo goo gai pan, "at first I thought you were leaping to all sorts of unfounded conclusions, imagining murder without a shred of proof, but now it seems you really were on to something from the very beginning."

"What do you mean?"

"When Derek died, you were the only one who believed it was anything but natural causes. And I couldn't understand why."

"I guess it was just my murderous intuition," I offered smugly, digging a fork into the shrimp fried rice, "gained from years of reading mystery novels."

Lee disagreed. "No, it had to be more than that. Somehow you knew—even when there wasn't a single fact supporting your position—you still knew."

I absently rubbed my left thumb. "I could just as easily have been wrong."

She laughed. "I thought you were. Even after Derek's autopsy, I still couldn't believe you had gotten it right. With absolutely nothing to go on. There has to be a reason. It can't just be coincidence or simple blind luck."

"Maybe there's a connection between some family members," I suggested seriously, "some sort of mystical bond that goes beyond logic, beyond the ability to explain or understand."

"You mean like the mother who wakes in the middle of the night certain her child is in some kind of danger? And the danger turns out to be real?" She took a big bite out of an egg roll.

I nodded my head. "Exactly."

"Well, if that's the case here, then who does your sixth sense tell you the killer is?"

"I wish I knew."

"Don't ask me how, but I think you do."

"You think I know who the murderer is?"

"Yes." Lee leaned toward me on the sofa. "The killer came after you. That means that somewhere along the way you met up with him face-to-face."

"Or her," I amended, squirting sweet-and-sour sauce over a slice of pork.

"Or her. But the point remains—if you just think about it—you know the name of the killer."

I laughed. "That's easy for you to say. And just how do you recommend I go about identifying him?"

"Or her?"

I smiled. "Or her?"

"Follow the basic rules of detective fiction."

"Ah," I murmured. "Means, motive, opportunity."

"Precisely."

I mused, crunching on a crispy water chestnut. "Well, the motive seems obvious. Money. Everybody I've met would qualify on that score. The means? In the case of the poisoned vitamins, it would require some specialized knowledge. But just about anyone at the Holcomb Company might possess that kind of information."

"What about opportunity, then?"

"If we're only considering the current murders, then that doesn't eliminate anybody. But if we include the deaths of John Holcomb and his family, then we'd only be looking for someone in his"—catching Lee's expression, I hastily added—"or her late fifties or older."

"Well," my wife asked after allowing me a minute's reflection, "has this helped any?"

I shook my head despondently and tossed the empty egg foo yung carton toward the wastebasket.

"Then maybe there's one other person you still need to interview. That is, if you're correct in your supposition."

"What are you talking about?" I asked in surprise. "Who do you mean?"

"Elizabeth Holcomb," Lee answered, then added softly, "your mother."

The Lansdale Sanitarium was located across the river from Louisville, in an unincorporated community known as Martinsville. The institution's main buildings were set well back from the road, surrounded by several acres of manicured lawns and gardens. Varying species of birch and pine trees dotted the pastoral landscape.

"I can definitely appreciate the calming influence of the place," Lee admitted as I turned the Mustang into the sanitarium's parking lot.

The drive out from the city had taken no more than an hour, but it had been a very long sixty minutes, in part because I had sulked most of the way. Before we left the loft, Lee had threatened divorce if I once again insisted on bringing Weezer along. I had finally deferred, but, I hate to admit it, not very graciously. However, by the time we pulled into the single parking space marked for visitors, I was over my pique and ready to talk.

"We need a plan," I announced as we headed toward the double-plated glass entrance.

"Why?"

"They're not just going to let us walk right in and see Elizabeth Holcomb, with no questions asked," I said. "And I can't go claiming she's my mother. We'd certainly get tossed out on our ear with that one."

"Why don't we just see what happens?" my wife suggested as she pulled open one of the doors.

The interior of the Lansdale Sanitarium conveyed the unmistakable aura of hospital neutrality. The walls were painted in an off-white drab, the inlaid-tile floor was peeled slippery from too many mandatory scrubbings, and the climatized air reeked from a toxic mixture of Pine-Sol and Clorox. My first impulse was to turn around and run back out into the fresh air and sunshine, and, I thought, the faster the better.

"May I help you?" The woman behind the barricaded front desk wore a white uniform and a plastic smile.

"Yes," Lee answered. "We'd like to see Elizabeth Holcomb."

The white uniform stiffened. "Miss Holcomb doesn't get many callers. In fact, in the fifteen years I've been here, she's only had one regular visitor that I know of." Her eyes narrowed suspiciously. "Are you members of her immediate family?"

I could have told her that Elizabeth Holcomb doesn't have any immediate family. Not anymore. But then I suspected she already knew that.

My wife gave the white uniform a withering look. "We're friends of the family," Lee announced haughtily. "Didn't Mr. Brevard inform you of our intended visit?" Lee sounded like Helen Hayes playing Queen Victoria, with a touch of Alexander Woollcott thrown in for good measure.

The white uniform wilted under my wife's superior gaze. "Well, I'll have to check with her attending psychiatrist first."

"We do not like to be kept waiting," Lee warned regally.

By this time the white uniform was quite definitely flustered, "I suppose I could take you to Miss Holcomb and then inform the doctor."

"Very good." I felt that Lee's clipped intonation was a bit over the top, but the white uniform seemed to be eating it up. She stepped from behind her protective shell. "This way, please."

Lee and I followed the white uniform mutely. I didn't dare say anything for fear of giving the game away. Once again my wife had astonished me with her thespian skills.

"Miss Holcomb should be in the sunroom," the white uniform volunteered. The long silent walk down the endless corridor must have been unnerving her.

"We have heard that Elizabeth has been ill." Lee deigned to speak. "Some sort of cancer?"

The white uniform shook her head decisively. "That's absolutely not true. I don't know how that rumor got started, but Miss Holcomb is in perfect physical health. And I assure you she receives absolute top-notch treatment here."

"I am sure." Lee's tone indicated neither affirmation nor denial. But the white uniform seemed more nonplussed than ever.

"I assure you, madam, Lansdale Sanitarium enjoys one of the finest reputations in the state." She pushed against a swinging door and ushered Lee and me through the opening. "And our doctors are the best in their—" She stopped in mid-sentence.

Directly ahead of us, against a solid wall of windows that revealed a lush outside greenery, a lone woman sat rocking idly in a wheelchair.

"Where's the attendant?" the white uniform demanded of no one in particular. "Miss Holcomb is never to be left alone."

"Is this how you run your hospital?" Lee said sternly. "I can assure you that Mr. Brevard will certainly hear of this outrage."

Clearly agitated, the white uniform offered profuse apologies. "I'm so sorry. Nothing like this has ever happened before. I can't understand it. I must get the doctor."

She hurried back toward the door, then hesitated for a brief moment, obviously uncertain whether the proper course of action was to go for assistance or to remain with her patient.

"Well?" Lee's imperious tone decided her. The white uniform disappeared through the swinging doors.

"You were marvelous," I gushed once we were alone with Elizabeth Holcomb.

"Never mind." Lee's voice was back to normal. "We don't have much time. It's your show now." She tilted her head toward the room's one other occupant.

I walked toward the woman in the wheelchair, unclear as to how I should feel, undecided as to what I should say. I reached her side, dropped to my knees, and looked into her unlined face.

Elizabeth Holcomb gave the appearance of being trapped in time, like a porcelain doll preserved for centuries under tempered glass. She possessed a near-ethereal beauty, and her skin exuded the translucent sheen of fine pearls. Her eyes, a blue so clear they seemed almost colorless, held a vacant stare. She continued to rock back and forth in her chair.

"Mother?" I couldn't believe I said that.

But Elizabeth Holcomb stopped in mid-rock and slowly turned her head, shifting her gaze from the vast abstract to the mere concrete. To me. To my face.

"Eric?" Her voice was barely a whisper, so thin and wispy it almost didn't register on the decibel scale. "Eric, is that you?" She lifted a shaking hand and brushed it lightly against my cheek. A single tear escaped from her right eye. "Where are Derek and Nan? Did they come with you?"

"What's going on here?" A man in a white smock stood framed in the doorway. "You people have no business being in here. Now, get out."

I stood up and cast a parting glance down at my mother. Her frail hand was still outstretched. I extended my right hand and lightly touched her fingers.

"If you don't leave now," the man threatened, "I'll have you thrown out." I didn't doubt his sincerity for a second.

Lee and I left more quickly and much less noticeably than we had come. Once we were safely back in the Mustang, Lee asked, "Kyle, what do you think? Is Elizabeth Holcomb your mother?"

I nodded. "Yes, I think so," I answered softly. "She called me Eric. That must have been the name she gave me at birth."

"How could she possibly know who you were? Supposedly she hasn't seen you since you were born. There's no way she could possibly recognize you now.

"Maybe Derek came to visit her just like we did? But then she would have called you Derek. How could she know you weren't?"

"I have no idea," I answered with a bewildered shake of my head. "It's a mystery to me. Nevertheless, she did call me Eric."

"What else did she say?" Lee persisted. "I couldn't hear a word."

I didn't respond to Lee directly. "If I'm Eric, and we know about Derek," I said distractedly, still puzzling the riddle around in my mind, "then who the hell is Nan?"

CHAPTER 17

*"This novel
provides
a good lesson
in anyone's mystery
education."*

—Stokes Moran,

on Elizabeth George's *Well-Schooled in Murder*

"Are you sure you heard her right?"

"Yes, I heard her right!" I said for perhaps the fourth time since Lee and I left the sanitarium.

It was now mid-afternoon, and we had once again returned to the loft to consider the possibilities. Lee continued to press the point that I knew more than I thought I knew, if I would just open up my mind. At the moment, though, I was feeling mulishly close-minded.

"What do you think it means, then?"

"What do I think it means?" I mimicked. "You sound just like Sigmund Freud. How the hell should I know what it means?"

"You must have some idea."

"Look," I complained, "you're not a psychiatrist, and I'm not lying on any couch." Actually, I was.

"Kyle, I'm not trying to psychoanalyze you, though I do think you're still in denial."

"Denial? Now what are you talking about?"

Lee leaned forward. "Just look at your actions. First, you denied Derek. You denied his existence, you denied he was your brother, you denied his claim that you were adopted, you denied his death—"

I interrupted. "I never denied Derek's death," I protested.

"Yes, you did." Lee pounded her fist impatiently. "Your single-minded obsession that he was murdered, even when there was no reasonable evidence to support it, allowed you to focus on something—anything—other than the fact that Derek was dead. You still have not come to terms with his death and how that makes you feel."

"That sounds like cheap psychobabble to me." I jeered dismissively.

Lee frowned, her eyes narrowing into reptilian slits. "You can call it whatever you like," she said angrily. "But somewhere inside that thick pigheaded skull of yours, you know I'm right."

I've often claimed that my wife knows me better than anyone. On this point, perhaps she even knew me better than I knew myself. While Lee sat silently fuming, I considered the possibility that she might be right when she claimed that my premature judgment of murder had nothing whatsoever to do with blood ties or gut feelings but merely had served as an excuse not to have to deal with the reality of Derek's death.

Maybe that had been my prime motivation all along—to delay the inevitable, to curb the emotions, to hide from the truth. I finally concluded that while I still didn't have all the answers, I was now at least willing to give Lee the benefit of the doubt.

"I'm sorry," I said.

Thankfully, Lee is not the kind of wife to hold a grudge. With her, a simple apology is all that's needed to scatter the clouds and bring back the sun.

She smiled. "Then you admit I'm right."

"Let's just say I concede the possibility." I laughed.

"Good," she said. "Now that we've got all that cleared up, what do you think Elizabeth Holcomb meant?"

I groaned. "Why are you back on that kick?"

"Because I want you to think it out."

"Well, the obvious conclusion is that there were three children instead of two."

Lee nodded. "That's what I think too. Triplets?"

Triplets? Triplets instead of twins? Was that possible? Memories of Ellery Queen's *The Finishing Stroke* flashed through my mind. Could it be?

"Nan might be from a later birth?" I suggested.

"I don't think so," Lee said. "From what you told me, Elizabeth Holcomb has been confined in that hospital almost since the time of her family's deaths."

"That's right."

"Then it's not likely she ever had more than one pregnancy," Lee continued. "That single time she was so conveniently indisposed. When you, Derek, *and* Nan were born. Or so we believe."

Point well taken.

Suddenly, I heard a scratching sound coming from inside the sofa, directly underneath where I sat. Within a second or two, Weezer's head tunneled out from between the seat cushions. Then, with a slight hoist, the little animal propelled the rest of her lithesome body into sight.

I laughed.

"Now, how did she do that?" Lee asked in astonishment.

I scooped Weezer up in my arms. "I guess this must be one of the hiding places Lowell was talking about, isn't that right, little one?" I playfully tossed the ferret into the air. She instantly splayed her legs, preparing, I suppose, for a rough landing, but I caught her with ease.

The telephone rang. Regrettably, I had left it on the kitchen table, so I propped Weezer up on my shoulder while I walked over to answer it. The little animal was just in the process of rappelling down the lofty heights as I wedged the receiver against my ear.

"I thought I told you to stay put." At first confusion, I thought the angry words were meant for the recalcitrant ferret, now attempting a high-wire walk down my left arm. "What did you think you were doing, going off to the Lansdale Sanitarium like that?"

Ah, Lieutenant Ricketts. Not only had I ignored his edict, I had also forgotten about the police surveillance.

"Good afternoon to you too," I said, setting Weezer safely on the floor. I watched her scurry over to her food dish.

"Don't try to soft-soap me." Now, why would I do that? "What the hell did you think you were doing?"

"You're repeating yourself, Lieutenant."

"Will you please give me a straight answer?" I'm pretty sure these last words exceeded his normal voice decibel range.

"Well, since you asked so nicely," I answered sweetly, "I was visiting my mother."

"Your mother?" He seemed momentarily befuddled. "You mean Elizabeth Holcomb?"

"One and the same."

"Why?"

"Why not?"

"Are you always this irritating?"

"Only on my good days."

"Look, just don't go anywhere. Despite the currently appealing prospect of having someone blow you away, I can't afford to have my men gallivanting all over kingdom come."

"I understand, Lieutenant."

"Then you'll stay put?"

"Certainly."

"Like bloody hell you will." The phone went dead in my ear.

"He hung up on me."

Lee laughed. "I can't say I blame him. When you get smugly sarcastic, believe me, I don't want to talk to you either."

I shrugged, joining her again on the sofa. "Suit yourself."

She reached over and lightly touched my hand. "He's a nice man, Kyle, and he's only trying to help. Now, why did you treat him so badly?"

"I don't know," I answered honestly. "I guess I just took my frustrations out on him."

"What frustrations?"

"Nothing turned out the way I expected. I thought I'd come down here, pretend to be Derek for a little while, smoke out the killer, and end up a hero."

Lee smirked. "You're lucky you're not a dead hero."

"I found out it's not easy impersonating someone," I continued, "even when he's your exact double. I know it didn't work as well with me and Derek as it did with *The Prince and the Pauper* or even with John and Monsieur le Comte."

"What are you talking about?" my wife asked in bewilderment. "And who's Monsieur le Comte?"

"He's the French bad guy in Daphne du Maurier's *The Scapegoat* who forced John, his English doppelgänger, to swap places. But the whole thing ended up being a very successful masquerade. It's one of my favorite books, and I sorta had the idea I could do the same."

"Well, I'm not sure I ever read that story," Lee admitted. "My favorite du Maurier character has always been Mrs. Danvers. She's so wonderfully evil. I really feel— Kyle, what's wrong? You look like you've just seen a ghost."

I felt drugged, thickheaded, dumbfounded. I slowly recovered from the thunderbolt. I had read about startling revelations; now I had experienced one. Lee had been right—I did have the answers, and all the pieces of the puzzle had suddenly fallen into place. With one completely innocent remark. Now I not only knew the identity of the killer, I also knew the identity of the next victim. I abruptly stood up.

"Let's go," I said urgently, then I started running toward the exit.

"Go where?" Lee scrambled to her feet, already half the

length of the room behind me. "Kyle, what's the hurry? What's happened?"

I stopped in the doorway. "I had the wrong book," I yelled, then bolted down the stairs, my wife now in hot pursuit.

CHAPTER 18

"No one ever said
that
being fair
was an absolute
requirement
for mystery fiction."

—Stokes Moran, on Susan Dunlap's *Death and Taxes*

"We're too late," I exclaimed.

The flashing blue lights of two police cars and a coroner's wagon greeted us as we pulled to a stop at the sanitarium's front entrance.

"You don't know that for sure," Lee cautioned, unbuckling her seat belt.

"Don't I?"

I leaped from the car and rushed frantically through the sanitarium's front doors, barely avoiding a head-on collision with two men propelling a gurney. I didn't need to ask the identity of the body lying under the white sheet. But I asked anyway.

"Elizabeth Holcomb?" I dreaded the anticipated answer. One of the attendants nodded.

"What happened?"

"Talk to the officer in charge."

"Officer in charge? Why are the police here?"

"The deputies always come out when we have a patient die. It's just a matter of routine."

"But—"

He frowned. "Look, you got any more questions, like I said, ask the officer in charge."

"Who would that be?"

"Gates, I think his name is." The attendant looked to his partner for confirmation, but the other attendant just shrugged. "Anyway, that's him over there talking to the nurse." The attendant inclined his head toward the reception desk. "Now if you don't mind, we've got to get this body to the morgue."

The urgency now passed, I waited for Lee to join me. We then approached the policeman together.

"Excuse me," I said when we were virtually standing at his elbow.

The officer and the nurse looked up in unison. The nurse suddenly shrieked, "That's them. The couple I told you about. They were the last ones to see Elizabeth Holcomb alive."

"Well, folks, I've been wanting to talk to you." The officer shot the nurse a triumphant look. "Why don't we all just come along back here and have a little sit-down?"

Lee squeezed my arm, a wifely warning to be cautious. But at the moment I didn't care if the officer thought I was Jack the Ripper. All I wanted was information.

"How did she die?" I asked, once the four of us had moved

into a vacant office and the officer had closed the door behind us.

"If you don't mind," he chided, "I'll ask the questions here. Now if you'll just sit down—"

"I don't want to sit down," I exploded. "I want to know what happened to my mother."

"Your mother?" the officer and the nurse chorused in surprise. Lee groaned.

"Yes, my mother." I knew I was being reckless, but I didn't care. "I don't have time to explain it all to you right now. Just tell me how she died."

"What's your name?" the officer asked, pulling a notebook and pencil from his shirt pocket.

"Kyle Malachi, but what's that got to do with anything?" He dutifully wrote it down.

He turned to my wife. "And yours?"

"My wife's name is Lee." I grabbed the notebook out of his hand. "None of that matters. Tell me how Elizabeth Holcomb died."

"I am trying to be patient," he said. "You don't seem to understand. This is a police investigation. Now, give me back my notebook."

Grudgingly, I complied. "Look, call Lieutenant Ricketts of the Louisville Police Department. He'll tell you everything you need to know."

"Lieutenant Ricketts?" The officer wrote that name down as well.

I struggled to control my temper. Since I was currently standing in the middle of a psychiatric hospital, I had a feeling if I vented my frustration I'd end up in a straitjacket.

"Please"—I clipped my words—"tell me what happened."

The officer sighed. "It looks like Elizabeth Holcomb had a heart attack."

"Your visit must have upset her," the nurse said, glaring resentfully at me. "It's your fault."

Everything that had thus far happened in this case had been my fault, so why should this tragedy be any different? There was a large part of me that agreed with the nurse.

"Look, Officer—" I inflected my voice into a question mark.

"Gates," he responded. "Deputy Gates."

"Look, Deputy Gates, I assure you that Elizabeth Holcomb was alive and well when we left her. And she did not have a heart attack."

"How can you know that?" he demanded.

I felt Lee tense next to me, but she remained silent. "Because Elizabeth Holcomb was murdered."

The nurse gasped, Lee stared at the ceiling, but Gates registered no surprise.

"We don't have any indication of foul play in Miss Holcomb's death," he said in his businesslike manner. "There'll be a routine autopsy, of course, but from all the preliminary indications it appears she died from natural causes."

"Tell the coroner to look for digitoxin poisoning," I said.

"Digitoxin poisoning?"

"Yes. That's the method the killer used to try to make Derek Winslow's death look like natural causes." I sarcastically stressed the last two words.

I turned to the nurse. "When we were here earlier, you mentioned Elizabeth Holcomb only ever had one regular visitor. Will you tell me that person's name?" I pleaded.

Affronted, the nurse bristled. "Of course, I won't do any such thing."

I turned back to the deputy. "Call Lieutenant Ricketts," I said. "He'll confirm that this is a murder, and that I have to have that name."

"Well, I don't know." For the first time, Gates seemed less than sure of his position. I felt I knew what he was thinking. As a deputy sheriff, he couldn't afford the political fallout if it turned out he had impeded a murder investigation.

I tried a different tack. "Let me have a pen and paper." Gates obligingly handed me his notebook and pencil. "I'm writing down the name of the individual I believe was Elizabeth Holcomb's visitor." I tore off the sheet of paper on which I had just recorded the name. "Ask the nurse to whisper the name to you. If what she says matches what I've written, will you then call Lieutenant Ricketts?"

Gates looked at the name on the paper, then he frowned. "I don't suppose it would hurt anything."

"You're not taking this man's claims seriously, are you?" objected the nurse.

"Look," he said, "if there's the slightest possibility that this woman was murdered, you wouldn't want to be accused of interfering with the police, would you?" Gates was transferring his worries onto the nurse. She didn't like the tether either.

"Well," she said. "I guess it'll be all right." She leaned over and whispered the name into the deputy's ear.

Gates folded the paper, walked over to the desk, and picked up the phone. He spoke into the receiver. "Get me the Louisville Police Department," he said. "A Lieutenant Ricketts."

I had my confirmation.

"Whose name did you write down on that paper?" Lee demanded excitedly once we were safely back in the Mustang. "And is that the killer?"

"Not now," I said abruptly.

I started the car's engine, anxious to get as far away from the Lansdale Sanitarium as quickly as I could. Lee didn't realize just how narrowly we had escaped being held as material witnesses in Elizabeth Holcomb's murder, as my most recent telephone encounter with Lieutenant Ricketts could attest.

"He wants to speak to you," Deputy Gates had said, handing me the receiver. Even though I had followed the deputy's side of the telephone conversation intently, I had been able to gather very little from Gates's numerous "I see"s and "uh-huh"s. After the deputy's initial explanation of why Gates was calling, Lieutenant Ricketts had done most of the talking.

"Are you deliberately trying to give me ulcers, or is this just the boneheaded way you always behave?" The lieutenant had shouted his first question.

I was fairly certain the question didn't require an answer, and, sure enough, Ricketts didn't wait for a response. "What are you doing out there again anyway?" he had continued without interruption. "I thought I told you to stay put."

"Well—"

"Never mind. If you're not careful, I'm going to tell that deputy to haul you in as a material witness. At least that way, I know you'll be out of trouble."

"But—"

"And out of my hair. Now, listen up. Sergeant Brent is on his way in. You forgot about the tail again, didn't you? I must say you're really racking up the mileage." Ricketts paused momentarily to catch his breath. "Well, Brent followed you to the sanitarium, and he's been sitting outside there for the past fifteen minutes wondering what the hell was going on."

"If—"

"I just radioed him"—Ricketts once again overruled my attempt to get a word in edgewise—"and instructed him to get his ass in there and resolve this situation before you turn it into an international disaster."

"I think—"

"I don't happen to give a rat's ass what you think. You just sit there and be quiet. Brent will handle everything. And if we're lucky, we might just all of us get out of this mess with our balls intact. Got it?"

"May I say something?"

"No." Ricketts slammed the phone down in my ear. I was becoming accustomed to the manner in which he ended his telephone conversations, but I still cringed at the explosive sound.

Deputy Gates looked at me expectantly. I merely shrugged and handed him back the receiver. Just then, a knock was heard at the door. Without waiting for an invitation, Sergeant Brent entered the office.

"Deputy Gates," he said. "I'm Lionel Brent, a sergeant with Louisville Homicide. I believe you just talked to Lieutenant Ricketts."

"That's right," Gates said. "Now, your lieutenant didn't give me much opportunity to speak, so I'll lay it out plain for you. This is Martinsville, and I'm afraid I'm going to have to tell Sheriff Perkins that the Louisville PD came into her county without proper authorization or even without letting her know. And I can tell you from personal experience, she's not going to be the least bit happy about it."

Brent walked over to where the deputy was standing. "I'm sure we can work this thing out," the sergeant said amicably. "And keep it just between us."

I nudged Lee. She glanced at me, and I gave a quick jerk of my head toward the door. She nodded her understanding. So, while the two lawmen were still wrangling over their territorial jurisdictions, Lee and I had eased from the office and made good our escape.

Without a minute to waste, I steered the Mustang down the hospital drive, through the gates, and out onto the highway. A mile down the road, I checked the rearview mirror. No vehicle of any kind was visible.

"Whew." I finally expelled the repressed air from my lungs. I smiled at Lee, dreading the thought of the inevitable dressing-down Sergeant Brent would surely receive, or my next certain-to-be-volatile encounter with Lieutenant Ricketts. But, for the moment, I had freedom of movement, and that's all that mattered.

"Now, what were you saying?" I asked my wife, once I had secured a safe five-mile cushion between us and the sanitarium.

"I only asked you what name you wrote down on that piece of paper. You didn't have to ignore me."

"I'm sorry," I apologized, checking the rearview mirror once again. "I just needed all my concentration to get us out of there before we both ended up in the local hoosegow."

She laughed, her mood broken. "You really think that was a possibility?"

"Oh yes," I answered. "More than you know."

"Well, we're safely away now. Do you think you can finally answer my question."

"And what question was that?"

"Oh, you." Lee playfully slapped my shoulder. "You know what the question is. For the third time," she sighed, "whose name did you write on that paper?"

"I wrote the name of Elizabeth Holcomb's mother," I answered simply.

"You mean Louise Holcomb?" Lee asked in astonishment. "But she's dead."

I shook my head. "Not Louise Holcomb."

Lee frowned. "I don't understand."

"Neither did I," I admitted. "For far too long."

"Okay," she laughed, "I can see you've got it all figured out, and that you're going to make me drag it out of you. So tell me. If not Louise Holcomb, then who?"

I smiled mysteriously at my wife, prolonging the suspense.

"Adelaide Crimm," I said at last. "My grandmother."

CHAPTER 19

"She has spent
much of her life
distancing
herself from the past,
but eventually
she is forced to come
face-to-face with the truth."

—Stokes Moran,

on Triss Stein's *Murder at the Class Reunion*

"You knew I wasn't Derek from the beginning, didn't you?"

Adelaide Crimm, her blue eyes still sparkling from the tears she had spilled during our long emotional embrace, nodded. "When you telephoned, even though you sounded like Derek, you called me Mrs. Crimm. The last time I saw Derek he was calling me Grandmother." Here her voice slightly faltered. "Just like you did a few minutes ago."

With Lee and me standing expectantly on her front porch, Adelaide Crimm had opened the door, a quizzical expression on her crinkled face. Not even allowing her an opportunity to speak, I had said softly, "Grandmother?" The next moments had been lost to me as I had surrendered to her desperate clinging.

Now she and I were sitting on the sofa in her living room, her hands fervently gripping mine. Lee perched on a nearby chair, her eyes moist with tears as well.

"Why did you go along with the deception?" I asked, perplexed. "Why didn't you just tell me you knew I wasn't Derek?"

"I guess I still wanted to keep my secrets," Addie sniffled. "I knew something bad must have happened to Derek, or else you wouldn't be pretending to be him. And I didn't want to make the same mistake again, so when you came to visit, I went along with your story."

"What did you mean when you said you didn't want to make the same mistake again? What mistake?"

Addie laughed. "I made an old lady's mistake with Derek," she said, wiping her left hand across her cheek. "He didn't call ahead like you did. He just showed up at the door one day, and I was so surprised that I accidentally called him by name."

I shook my head. "How did you know who he was?"

"That's what Derek wanted to know too." She laughed again. Addie rose from the sofa, walked slowly and stiffly over to an antique highboy that stood against the far wall, opened one of its drawers, and pulled out what appeared to be several loose-leaf scrapbooks.

"You see," she said, opening the cover of the top book, "I've been keeping track of you boys all your lives. She turned to the back of the scrapbook and held the page so I could see. "I had no trouble recognizing Derek."

I glanced down at the book. A head-and-shoulders shot of Derek dominated a story announcing his departure from the *Louisville Courier.*

"I probably could have covered my mistake just by saying I recognized him from the newspaper," Addie said. "But I think I really wanted him to know the truth. And after forty years, I wanted to be able to hug my grandson once again." This time she sobbed audibly and reached to embrace me again.

"Derek left you his diary, didn't he?" I asked, gently stroking her hair.

Addie moved her head against my chest, indicating assent, then she pushed herself upright. "Yes," she said, "he told me he wanted it in safe hands."

"And the vitamins?"

Addie laughed, a puzzled expression clouding her face. "How did you know that?"

"Doesn't matter."

"Oh, but it does." She misunderstood my words. "Like I told Derek, those vitamins are the reason you're here. They brought John Holcomb into my life."

"I wish you could have met Johnny," Addie said, retreating into the past. "He was the most wonderful man I've ever known."

"Tell me."

She smiled and patted my hand. "You couldn't tell it now, but I cut a fine figure once. And so full of myself. I didn't think any of the local boys were good enough for me. That's why I was still unmarried at the ripe old age of twenty-five the summer John Holcomb came looking for mountain remedies, the summer of '37." Addie's eyes slowly acquired a faraway look.

"I still lived with my mama. Papa was already gone by that time, rest his soul, and all my brothers and sisters had long been married and gone off to establish their own homes. So it was just me and Mama.

"Now, my mama was a real mountain granny. And I hope you understand that by granny I mean a kind of medicine woman. All the local folk came to her for healing potions and salves, and I guess I caught a little of the magic from her. I never was as good with the remedies as she was, but I knew enough to keep from killing anybody."

Addie laughed, pulled a handkerchief from her skirt pocket, and dabbed her nose.

"Of course, as fate would have it, John Holcomb somehow heard about Mama. He had come to the mountains to buy timber rights, but—I learned this about him later—he also had a genius for chemistry. So basically it was his scientific curiosity that eventually brought him to Mama. But the minute I set eyes on Johnny, I knew he was the man for me.

"The only problem was, he was already married. I didn't care that he was more than ten years older than me, or that he was from the big city, or even that he was rich. None of that mattered. But I did care that he had a wife. You see, back in those days, good girls just didn't mess with a man who wore a wedding ring. And even though I was independent-minded and headstrong, I was very definitely a good girl.

"Johnny spent that whole summer in the mountains, most of the time with me. He used to tell me that it was the best time of his life. You can't imagine how free we were. Of course, I didn't appreciate what it meant to Johnny. Free from the pressures of his business, free from the problems of his family, Johnny was more alive than anyone I had ever encountered. And he made me feel alive too, just being around him.

"We went everywhere together. Digging for herbs, picking berries, cooking up many of Mama's medicinal recipes. Johnny taught me about the wonders of life, the miracles of chemistry. We experimented with all kinds of different concoctions, and that's when we hit on the formula for the vitamins I gave to Derek. I guess I even felt a little bit like Madame Curie. Working shoulder to shoulder with the man I loved.

"Oh, and I did love him. There was no mistaking that. And I felt he loved me too. But we both knew nothing must ever come of it.

"So Johnny left at the end of that summer, with enough of Mama's secrets to start a drug company. And I let him go, even though my heart was broken. I didn't think I'd ever see him again. The tall handsome man with the crooked smile." Addie lifted her hand and touched my lips. "Not so very different from you.

"But Johnny wouldn't leave it at that. That October, he came back. Said his life meant nothing, that he couldn't live without me. Of course, I ate it all up." Addie laughed self-consciously, twisting the handkerchief in her hand into a small ball. "It's what I wanted to hear.

"I hadn't expected Johnny that day. Mama had gone off to tend to a sick neighbor, and we were alone together. I had spent a miserable time since he had been gone. I have no excuses, I'm not even sure I wanted any," she said, speaking so softly I could hardly catch the next three words. "We made love."

Addie blushed at the recollection, or the admission, I wasn't sure which.

"Johnny left before Mama got back, and I didn't tell her he had ever been there. He promised he'd get a divorce as soon as possible and come back for me. I believed him, and I think he believed his promises too.

"Christmas came, then New Year's. Johnny had written almost every day, but never with any definite schedule as to when we would be together. Then I suddenly realized time was running out.

"I knew enough about women's things to recognize I was pregnant. I wrote to Johnny and told him he was about to become a father. No letter came in return.

"I was frantic, terrified. I knew if I told Mama, she'd give me something to get rid of the baby. And I wanted desperately to keep the child, Johnny's child.

"Two weeks after I'd written that last letter, Johnny showed up, told Mama his wife had died, and that he wanted to marry me. In Louisville. Mama didn't object. After all, I was past the marrying age."

Addie smiled. "Johnny had lied, of course. I found that out once we were safely out of the mountains. He had made the whole story up just so my reputation wouldn't be ruined.

"He found me a little house outside Lexington. Far enough away from the mountains so that no one would find out, and far enough away from his home so that no one there would find out either. I didn't know what to think. To tell you the truth, I really didn't think. I had Johnny, and that's all that seemed to matter. When the time came for the baby, Johnny found an experienced midwife for me. Then, after the baby was born, Johnny took Elizabeth into his home to raise as his child, and later he brought me in as the housekeeper."

"That's terrible." Lee's sudden outburst startled both Addie and me.

"No, it's not," Addie said softly. "It's a price I gladly paid."

"But to deny you your own child," my wife said, then glared at me angrily. "That's a man for you."

"No, sweet thing," Addie comforted. "It's the only way it could work. Johnny had worked it all out very carefully."

"But why would his wife go along with such a thing?" Lee asked. "I wouldn't."

"Johnny held a secret over Louise's head," Addie answered. "He had married her to give a name to another man's child. I don't know the exact details, but now it was payback time. Johnny told Louise how things would be, and she went along."

Lee shook her head. "I still can't believe it."

Addie smiled. "Louise was not a strong woman, plus she was a little bit too fond of her whiskey. All she wanted from Johnny was comfort and position. Oh yes, she never voiced an objection."

Addie's tone suddenly acquired a harsher edge. "But Louise didn't do any more than she had to. She went along with the fiction that she was pregnant, she remained secluded in her house the last few months leading up to Elizabeth's birth, she played the public role of attentive new mother. But privately, it was the child who suffered. Elizabeth didn't understand why she was denied Louise's love."

"This sounds like something out of *Wuthering Heights*," commented my wife.

"I know it all seems ridiculous to you," Addie agreed, nervously kneading the handkerchief. "But, living it as I did, it seemed the only right thing to do. I had Johnny, and I had my daughter. Even if she couldn't know I was her mother, I still gave her all the love I had."

"Why don't you say something?" Lee challenged me to comment.

"So tell me about John Holcomb's death," I said to Addie.

"That was the worst time of my life," Addie said. "And it was all Robert's fault."

"Robert was Louise's son, right?"

Addie nodded. "Legally, he was Johnny's son too. And, of course, neither of the children was ever told they weren't brother and sister. That's how they grew up, and that's how it should have remained."

Addie coughed.

"I'm sorry," I said. "You've been doing all the talking. Could I get you a glass of water or something?"

Addie shook her head. "No, thank you. I'm fine." She continued the story. "But Robert was a bad boy, had always been a difficult child. I think he had a touch of Satan in him.

"I hate to say this, but I never liked him. But, even from the start, he doted on his younger sister. You see, Robert was four years old when Elizabeth was born. And as she grew up, Elizabeth absolutely adored her dashing older brother.

"Johnny was pleased with the way the children got along.

He never told me, but I don't think he ever much cared for Robert either. At least not until Elizabeth came along. But the boy was so different with her, so attentive, so solicitous, that Johnny thought he had a new son.

"But I never trusted Robert, not even then. Maybe I was jealous of the place he held in Elizabeth's heart, I don't know. All I do know is, something wasn't right with the boy.

"And when Elizabeth started maturing, I had my answer. I could see the lust lurking in Robert's eyes. He tried to disguise it, but he couldn't hide the truth from me.

"Of course, he was nineteen at the time, and had finally gone off to college. I can't tell you what a relief I felt to see him leave the house. But while he was away, Elizabeth had started to develop a figure.

"It was Christmas. Robert had only been gone for four months, but Elizabeth had really fleshed out in that short time. I could tell the moment Robert walked in the door we were in for trouble. The way he looked at his sister, it made my blood run cold.

"The day before he was due to head back to school, Robert announced that he wanted to stay at home and work for his father. Johnny was pleased at the boy's sudden interest in the business, and readily agreed. But I sensed what Robert had in mind, and I did everything I could to keep Robert and Elizabeth apart. She was only fifteen, and not yet at all wise in the ways of the world.

"But even my best efforts weren't sufficient to thwart Robert's evil intentions. On Valentine's night, he convinced Johnny to let him escort Elizabeth to the country club dance. Elizabeth was so excited—it was to be her first ball gown, her first grown-up social—my objections were quickly overruled. By both Johnny and Elizabeth.

"Of course, if I had confided my fears to Johnny, he might have acted differently. But back in those days, you didn't dare think such things, let alone speak them.

"So I watched the children leave, hoping against hope that my fears were unfounded.

"They weren't. Four months later, Elizabeth's unexplained illness was diagnosed as pregnancy—fortunately, Johnny was able to buy the doctor's silence—and Elizabeth finally admitted what had happened. But she still defended Robert, constantly weeping and proclaiming her undying love for him.

"Johnny was ready to kill the boy. It was all I could do to keep him rational. Louise was no help; she stayed so drunk most of the time that she rarely knew what was happening around her.

"It was a terrible summer. The whole household was in turmoil. Finally, I convinced Johnny to let me take Elizabeth away. He eventually agreed, making all the arrangements himself.

"Ironically, he sent us to the same little house outside Lexington where Elizabeth had been born. And when the time came, the same midwife came to help. But this time it was three babies instead of one." Addie smiled at me. "And before I could even think what to do with three children, Johnny died. Robert and Louise too."

Here Addie stopped her narrative. She looked at me with fresh tears in her eyes. She unrolled the handkerchief and wiped them away.

"You didn't tell me how he died," I prompted after a minute's silence.

"I don't know what happened," Addie finally admitted. "All the reports said it was an accident."

Again, she stopped.

"But you don't believe that, do you?"

Addie shook her head. "Under the circumstances," she continued, "Johnny would never have taken Louise and Robert on a holiday outing. He could barely stand being in the same house with them, let alone the three of them together on a small boat. No, I think Johnny was so sick of life that he left it willingly, and, God forgive him, played God with Louise and Robert as well."

"What about Lawrence Brevard?" I asked quietly. "Did he know about Robert and Elizabeth? Did he suspect what Johnny had in mind?"

Addie looked confused. "I don't understand. Lawrence Brevard?"

"Yes," I persisted. "Lawrence Brevard. Louise's brother. Johnny's brother-in-law. Was that why he got thirty percent of the company? To keep him quiet?"

Addie shook her head. "I don't know. I'm sorry. Maybe he did suspect, maybe he did say something to Johnny. I just don't know."

Once again, my grandmother fell silent. This time I granted her the privilege.

CHAPTER 20

"The novel
achieves near-perfect
pitch,
striking all
the right chords
along the way."

—Stokes Moran, on Linda Barnes's *Steel Guitar*

"Did you tell Derek all this?" I asked Addie, handing her a glass of water I'd fetched from the kitchen.

"Some of it," she said, taking a sip of the water. "Not all of it, though. Mostly we spent a wonderful afternoon together just coming to know each other. I didn't even tell him about you until he asked me point-blank if he had a twin. Then, what could I do? I didn't want to tell him a bald-faced lie after all these years."

"And you also told him how to find me, didn't you?" I reclaimed my seat on the sofa.

"Oh yes." Addie placed the water glass on a coaster and

picked up one of the scrapbooks. "This one is yours," she said with a smile. "I'm sorry Derek didn't get to see the albums, but we were having such a good time getting acquainted I never thought to show him. He would have enjoyed reading your reviews." She handed me the book with the blue cover. "After he had gone, I wished I had told him more about his past. I especially wish it now," she added wistfully. "As I get older, I find it's the things we don't say, more than the things we do, that we live to regret. You know what I mean?"

I leafed through the browned pages. Addie had assembled quite a hodgepodge of material. The earliest entry was an essay I'd written as a junior in high school, clipped from my hometown newspaper. I'd won fifty dollars for those five hundred words and had immediately spent the money on a dozen mystery novels, mostly Crime Club titles, if I recalled. I smiled, thinking even then the die—my love of mysteries—had been cast.

The next few pages covered various events from my college years—debate results, articles I'd written for the campus newspaper, my graduation picture. I'd forgotten how gangly and awkward I'd looked back then.

Then came my reviews, page after page of neatly clipped articles, the early ones bearing the Kyle Malachi byline, but most published under the Stokes Moran pseudonym I've employed for the past few years as a syndicated mystery columnist. I closed the book with an unexplained sense of contentment.

"How—" I started.

Addie interrupted. "How did I know who you were?" She

asked the question for me. "I never didn't know," she said, providing the answer as well.

"I don't understand."

She smiled. "When the babies were born, I had no idea how we'd cope with three children, but I knew somehow we would. Johnny would find a way. Then Johnny died, and I was completely lost.

"Even then, I probably would have kept the children together had Elizabeth been stronger. But she had always been very fragile emotionally. The past year had been very traumatic for her, it had been a difficult birth, and she was barely over that crisis when she found out about Robert's death. She went over the edge.

"There are medical terms for her condition, and, believe me, I've heard them all over the past forty years. Each succeeding psychiatrist gave it a different spin—paranoid schizophrenia, multiple personality disorder, manic-depression. In my day, we'd simply say Elizabeth lost her mind.

"Well, there I was, my beloved Johnny dead, Elizabeth unstable and most of the time completely hysterical, and three new babies on my hands. I decided the only sensible course of action available to me was to find new homes for the three of you."

"Eric, Derek, and Nan," I said.

Addie looked at me in amazement. "How did you know that?"

"I saw my mother today."

At first, Addie's face registered shock, then pleasure. "You did? How did she seem? I go every Sunday. Some times she's fine, other times she doesn't even know who I am."

Addie would soon enough learn of her daughter's death

through the normal channels, and I decided I would not be
the one to break the news.

"She was fine," I lied, then abruptly changed the subject.
"Tell me, were Derek and I joined at birth?" I consciously
rubbed my thumb.

She laughed. "Oh yes. The midwife and I had a dreadful
time with that. Your head popped out first, then your shoulders, but your left arm seemed caught on something. The
midwife worked and worked to get you out. I was afraid she
was going to break you in half the way she was pushing and
pulling. But eventually she had your little body out, all except
for the left hand. The midwife gave a final pull, and not only
did your hand come free, Derek slid right out too.

"That was the first we knew it was a multiple birth. Nan
came out a few minutes later."

Addie reached for the glass and downed a large gulp of water.
"What happened then?"

"The midwife took a kitchen knife and carefully severed
the connection between you and Derek." The sensitive skin
covering the old stump on my thumb suddenly throbbed in
sympathy.

My grandmother saw me rubbing my thumb and laughed.
"Oh, don't worry. It was over in a flash, and didn't seem to
hurt you or Derek a bit. And the way the three of you were
already exercising your lungs, we knew we had a healthy set
of babies on our hands."

"When did you decide to give us up for adoption?" I asked,
acknowledging to myself, for what was really the first time,
the true facts of my birth.

"You were about four weeks old, and it wasn't so much a

decision as it was an opportunity. This newly married couple lived next door to that little house in Lexington, and during the previous couple of months I had gotten quite friendly with the young bride. Her name was Paula." Addie smiled. "I think you might remember her."

Paula Malachi. The woman I'd always regarded as my mother. Yes, indeed I remembered her.

"Well, Paula and David seemed the perfect solution to my problem. She had already been told by her doctor that she could never have children of her own—some female thing—and they were both thrilled with the idea of adoption. Only thing"—Addie shook her head sadly—"they felt they couldn't take but one of the children. I tried my best to convince them otherwise. I think Paula would have gone along, no matter what the obstacles, but David was a more practical man. And he held firm.

"So I gave you to the Malachis. Please forgive me, but I thought it was for the best."

I wasn't sure forgiveness was even an issue. I had never felt cheated out of anything, never felt deprived of parental love or support. My growing-up years had been good. Yes, I had endured the normal loneliness of the only child, and maybe now I better understood my mother's temperamental possessiveness and my father's characteristic standoffishness. But I doubted I had suffered so bad a fate that it required forgiveness.

"There's nothing to forgive," I said softly.

Addie, newly sprouted tears shining in her eyes, patted my knee. "You're very kind, but I'm not so sure you're right. Either you or Derek. You see, I kept Nan."

"I left Derek on the steps of the Baptist orphanage chapel in Lexington," Addie continued. "With a little note giving his first name and date of birth. I knew he would be well taken care of, better than I could do certainly. You see, I didn't have any experience with boys. I was more comfortable with little girls."

Addie laughed, but it was a self-mocking kind of laughter. "I suppose Derek suffered the most. He didn't get a family until he was four years old. I checked on him every year. I felt tremendous guilt each time they told me he had still not found a home.

"And it wasn't like I intended to keep Nan. It just turned out that way."

I looked across the room and caught Lee's eyes. What thoughts were currently swirling around in my wife's feminist mind? I had a feeling we now had plenty of fodder for a score of *Oprah*s and *Geraldo*s.

"Once you were with the Malachis and Derek was at the orphanage, I left Nan with the midwife while I took Elizabeth back to Louisville. I consulted with several doctors and finally placed her at the Lansdale Sanitarium. At the time, I had no idea she'd never improve, that she'd remain there for the rest of her life.

"Then I went back to Lexington, intending, I believed, to find a home for Nan. But about that same time, I learned that Johnny had left me a good deal of money in his will. With the first check, I bought this house and moved Nan here with me, to raise as my own child."

Addie, her story spent, looked at me for reaction. I leaned over and planted a kiss on her cheek. She reached her arms around my neck, and I could feel her sobbing against my chest.

"I did the best I knew how," she said, her voice muffled against my body. "May God forgive me."

"Lee and I have to leave," I said, extricating myself from Addie's embrace.

"So soon?" she protested, sitting upright once again. "Becky should be home shortly, and I'd like to introduce you properly to your niece."

"Becky is Nan's daughter?" I inquired, rising to my feet.

"Yes, poor child. Nan died a little after Becky was born. Complications from childbirth, I'm afraid. And just like her mother and grandmother, without benefit of marriage."

Addie took my proffered hand and rose from the sofa. "I'm afraid we're not a very conventional family. I hope you don't mind."

Not very conventional? That had to be the biggest under-statement of all time. This family was almost biblical in its convolutions.

Lee, handbag in hand, already stood poised at the door. As Addie and I made our slow progress toward her, my wife opened the door for our exit.

I had one last question for Addie before Lee and I departed. "How were you able to give Derek my current address?"

Addie laughed. "I own the controlling interest in the New Albany newspaper. We carry your reviews."

"Talk about a potboiler!" Lee exclaimed once we were back in the car. "Addie's story would make a whale of a television miniseries."

I nodded, hopefully indicating with my reticence that I'd prefer not to talk just now. Lee took the hint, and we spent the remainder of the drive back into Louisville in singular silence.

"When you told me it was Addie's name you'd written down on that piece of paper," Lee said, standing on the threshold outside the loft while I fished in my pocket for Derek's key, "I thought you meant Addie was the killer. But I can't see that sweet little old lady murdering anyone."

When I inserted the key in the lock and turned, I found that the bolt was not engaged. With our hasty departure, Lee and I—really me; after all, it was my responsibility—had failed to secure the door.

"No, Addie's not the killer," I said, pocketing the needless key and pushing against the door. "I never even considered her a serious suspect." I ushered Lee through the open doorway.

"No," I continued, "what had bothered me about this case all along was how did Derek manage to identify me as his brother? I had no trouble understanding how he reached the conclusion that Elizabeth Holcomb was his mother. In fact, I was able to follow the same trail. But, at that point, it dead-ended. There was no possible link to me at all. Not unless somebody provided it. And, of all the people I'd met in the past three days, Addie seemed to be the only logical bridge between Derek and me. As long as she turned out to be Elizabeth Holcomb's mother, that is, and not her murderer."

"But you know who the killer is, don't you?" Lee asked, following me through the door.

"Oh yes. There's only one person it can be."

"Kyle, did you leave the lights on in the sitting area?"

"No, of course not. You can't leave the lights on. They're controlled by pressure sensors in the floor."

"Well, they're on. Look over there."

Lee was right as usual. Not only was the area of the room in which we were now standing awash in light, so too was the area around the sofa. Then those lights abruptly went out.

"We've got company," I said redundantly, half expecting to see Lieutenant Ricketts round the corner of the center block. But it was not the good lieutenant who produced the angry outburst I heard as Lee and I approached the center of the room.

"I hate these damn lights. I don't know how you stand them."

Becky Crimm stood framed in the spotlight, her right hand extended, a large gun aimed directly at my heart.

CHAPTE**R** 21

"It comes off the bat
like a tornado
and
knocks the nearest competition
completely out of the
ballpark."

—Stokes Moran, on Alison Gordon's *Night Game*

"Hello, Becky," I said.

"You don't seem surprised to see me," she answered.

"Well," I said, walking toward her, "I wasn't expecting to find you here."

"Don't come any closer," she warned.

Lee, pulling on my shoulder, whispered, "Kyle? What are you doing? She's got a gun."

"You don't mind if we sit down, do you, Becky?" I politely inquired.

"Just stay where you are!" she shouted, backpedaling toward the sofa. "Don't come any closer! I've already tried twice to kill you. Don't bet on your luck holding out a third time."

Half dragging Lee with me, I continued to face Becky's nervously bobbing gun. "Look, it's been a long day, and I'm tired. I'm going to have a seat."

Boy, had it ever been a long day. I was astonished to realize that it had been less than twelve hours since I had picked Lee up at the airport. In fact, it seemed like I had been in Louisville itself for three months instead of only three days.

"Listen to me!" Becky screamed, waving the gun wildly. "I'm going to shoot."

"Are you?" I asked mockingly. "I don't think so. Direct confrontation is not your style, Becky. You're more into natural causes and traffic accidents. Anyway, if you shoot, you might not get the money."

"Kyle, you're making her crazy!" Lee hissed urgently in my right ear, but I ignored my wife's latest news bulletin, rigidly fixing my attention instead on the gun in the killer's hands.

Becky's emerald eyes narrowed. "Money? What money?"

"Oh, come off it, Becky. We both know this whole thing's been about the money." I calmly crossed my legs and leaned back against the cushions.

"I don't know what you're talking about, Derek."

"Derek? I'm not Derek," I proclaimed with a teasing smile. "I'm Kyle."

"Kyle? But Kyle's in—" She stopped.

"Kyle's in Connecticut?" I finished for her. "Is that what you were going to say, Becky? Well, you're half right. I was in Connecticut. Until Derek paid me a visit, that is. But now I'm here." I stretched, raising my arms over my head and lacing the fingers of my hands together behind my neck. "And I'm ready to claim my inheritance."

"How—"

"You shouldn't feel too much a failure, Becky," I interrupted. "Your first two attempts weren't as unsuccessful as you think. You got Derek just like you planned. That's why I pretended I was Derek, so I could catch his killer. So I could catch you."

"You pretended to be Derek?"

I nodded. "Your grandmother knew. Or, should I say, your great-grandmother. In fact, we've just come from visiting Addie, and she admitted that she knew I was Kyle all along. Strange she didn't tell you," I suggested portentously. "I wonder why."

"Then the vitamins—" Becky stopped in mid-sentence, too late to cover her mistake.

I seized on the opening she provided. "Ah yes, I know all about the vitamins. Tell me, how did you manage to get the poison in the vitamins without Derek finding out?"

"Why should I tell you anything?"

"Why shouldn't you? You're planning on killing us anyway. So who would we tell?"

Just like all the fictional villains I've ever read about, Becky couldn't resist explaining her methods.

"I managed to intercept Derek's telephone call to the house," she said matter-of-factly. "I knew who he was, but at that time he didn't have any idea who I was or, more to the point, who Gran was. So I gave him some song-and-dance routine about not knowing anything when he asked about the Holcombs. And, after I hung up, I thought I had deterred him." She paused for a second, but I didn't interrupt her flow.

"But I guess I didn't do too well, because when I came home the next day, Derek was just leaving. And I was just in time to see Gran give him the vitamins, but luckily without either one of them seeing me. Believe me, I knew all about those vitamins, having been force-fed them all my life, and I knew what I had to do.

"So the next day, which just happened to be a Sunday, when I knew Gran would be away, I got another bottle and doctored four capsules with the digitoxin that I'd already made."

"Just how did you manage that?" I asked.

"It was simple," Becky bragged. "I just took a twenty-seven-centimeter syringe, inserted the needle into the capsules, drew out the vitamin mixture, and replaced that with the digitoxin, then I resealed the capsules with warm gelatin. It was easy."

Easy. And deadly.

"Then I drove over here," Becky continued, "knocked on Derek's door, and introduced myself simply by saying Addie had sent me to invite him for dinner the following Sunday. I felt it was a relatively harmless risk since I thought he'd be dead by then. I didn't want Derek to know who I really was, but just in case he mentioned my visit to Gran, I did give him my correct name. Of course, I hoped Derek would never get the chance to talk to Gran again, but if he did, I knew I could fool Gran into believing the invitation had been just a thoughtful gesture on my part." Becky stopped, seemingly to catch her breath for a moment, then she continued.

"I can't tell you what a scare you gave me yesterday," she admitted, "when I walked into Gran's house and found you there. At the time, I still thought you were Derek, of course, and I was just sure you'd give me away. But you played along just beautifully."

Yeah, Becky'd gotten all the breaks. Even my pretending to be Derek had played right into her hands, forcing me to accept her little charade without question. I had been too ignorant to know better. I shook my head, then directed my attention back to Becky, who continued with her explanation.

"And I was also a little bit concerned that Gran had already told him about me," Becky said. "But I realized right away that Derek didn't have the slightest idea who I was. He didn't question my presence at all, and after a little get-acquainted small talk, I asked to use his bathroom, and what do you think I found sitting right there in his medicine cabinet, just where I'd hoped they'd be?"

Becky smirked. "The vitamins. I removed four capsules from his bottle and replaced them with the ones I'd brought. It was as simple as that."

She frowned, then proceeded with her story. "Of course I couldn't run the risk of taking all but the four out of his bottle. He might have noticed. So I placed the poisoned ones on top, trusting that it wouldn't be too long before he took one.

Then, when I came out of the bathroom, I made up some excuse about having to get back to class so he wouldn't have time to ask me any questions, kissed him good-bye"—here Becky winked at me—"and went on my merry way."

"Ingenious," I complimented her with sarcasm. "Those poisoned capsules were just like four little time bombs waiting to explode. With no possible connection to you. Derek's death would have looked for all the world like a heart attack.

Except for one little thing." I felt my voice deepening with rage. I fought to keep my temper under control.

"What do you mean? What one little thing?"

"You didn't fool me. I knew Derek had been murdered, just like Addie knew it—even if she wouldn't admit it—when she realized I was impersonating Derek. And somewhere deep in her soul, Addie knows you're the one responsible. So if you're hoping for her help in proving your claim to the Holcomb inheritance, you can forget it. I assure you Addie will never go along with murder."

"I don't know what you're talking about." Becky attempted wide-eyed denial.

"Get off it, Becky. You're too smart to play dumb. You've already killed three people, now you're ready to make it five. So you might as well come clean. As they say, confession's good for the soul."

Lee pressed her lips next to my right ear. "Why are you baiting her like this?" she asked in a whisper.

I resisted my wife's caution and continued to address Becky. "If you think you can kill us and make it look like an accident, then you're very much mistaken. You've got police in three states working on the case right now. You might as well face the truth. Even if you succeed in killing us, you'll still never get your hands on that money. More likely, you'll end up spending the rest of your life in prison."

"I wouldn't be so sure of that if I were you."

"Oh really? If I could figure it out, I'm sure the police can."

Becky laughed derisively. "I don't believe you figured anything out. If I hadn't shown up tonight with a gun, you'd never have given me a second thought."

"If that's true, then there's no way I could know that you were Elizabeth Holcomb's attendant at the Lansdale Sanitarium today."

Becky's mouth dropped open. "How—"

"Was it just luck you were out of the room when we got there, or did you see us coming?"

"I—"

"It really doesn't matter. I also know you planted the false rumor about Elizabeth Holcomb's cancer. Or maybe you even started the rumor out as heart disease. But you know how unreliable secondhand information can be. It can get so twisted around."

I smiled at her conspiratorially. "You weren't in any hurry, of course. You had the whole summer to slowly feed Elizabeth Holcomb your special mix of poison, until eventually her heart just gave out. But when you saw us there today, you decided you couldn't afford to wait. So you gave her a massive dose, didn't you, and it was bye-bye Elizabeth.

"Tell me," and this time I couldn't quite keep the explosive anger clear of my voice, "do you enjoy killing your relatives? Should I warn Addie that she might be next?"

"You son of a bitch," she screamed, backing up against the window, "I'm going to enjoy killing you. And I don't care if it does look like murder. Now, stand up, or do you want it sitting down?" She coldly leveled the gun at my head.

"Kyle!" Lee yelled frantically. "She's going to shoot."

I heard the cock of the pistol. Then everything happened all at once. Weezer scampered across Becky's shoes. Startled, she fell backward, the gun coming up over her head and shattering the window behind her. Then, like a mote of dust caught up in a suction, Becky hurtled headlong through the broken glass.

But the image I remember most vividly from that moment is little Weezer, standing on her hind legs, her front feet braced against the window ledge, sniffing the air Becky had so recently vacated.

"Kyle, why were you sparring with her like that?" Lee demanded, just as I ended my brief call to 911. "She could have killed you."

"For one thing, I didn't think we had anything to lose. Becky just didn't drop in to say hello. She came here with every intention of murdering us. And for another, I was hoping we might throw her off balance."

Lee laughed. "Well, Weezer certainly did that."

I reached down and swept the precious little animal up in my arms. "I think it's delicious irony. Weezer exacts revenge on the murderer of her owners. Derek and Lowell would have loved the fact that Weezer was the instrument of Becky's destruction. Who'd ever think this tiny creature could bring down a diabolical killer."

"How long before the police get here?" Lee asked, applying fresh gloss to her lips.

"The 911 dispatcher said a unit should be here in about five minutes." I walked over to the window and looked down at Becky's lifeless body, fifty feet below. My, how the mighty had fallen. I grinned, and rubbed my nose against the ferret's fur.

"Tell me," Lee said, her cosmetic touch-up complete, "how did you figure out it was Becky?"

I turned away from the window. "Several reasons," I answered. "One, Becky was a direct-line descendant and, as such, could make a strong claim on the estate, especially if there were no other contenders. Two, she was in premed, so she had the expertise to rig the poison. Three, she had a summer apprenticeship at some nearby hospital, and it didn't require a degree in higher mathematics for me to come up with the Lansdale Sanitarium as the correct place."

"But you had no way of knowing she was John Holcomb's great-granddaughter," Lee objected.

"Sure I did," I responded. "You told me."

Lee gasped. "I told you? Whatever do you mean?"

I nodded. "You remember when we were talking about Daphne du Maurier, and you said Mrs. Danvers was your favorite character?"

"Yes," Lee answered with a frown, then her face suddenly cleared. "Oh, I see. Yes, Mrs. Danvers was the housekeeper, so that—" Her face clouded again. "No, I don't see. If Mrs. Danvers had reminded you of anyone, it would have been Addie since she had been John Holcomb's housekeeper."

"You're not thinking," I teased in a singsong taunt. "What did I yell at you right after that as I went barreling out the door?"

"Some fool thing about having the wrong book," Lee answered irritably.

"Well?"

"Well what?" Lee punched me in the stomach. "Stop playing these silly games with me."

"I had been talking about *The Scapegoat,* remember?" I explained. "So when I said I had the wrong book, I meant I had the wrong du Maurier."

Lee rubbed her hand across her eyes and nodded. "I have been dense," she admitted. "Of course I should have realized—*Rebecca*."

I smiled. "Exactly. It was like somebody suddenly turned on a lightbulb inside my brain. And once I was pointed in Becky's direction, everything else just sort of fell into place."

"But how did you know Elizabeth Holcomb was in immediate danger?"

"Elizabeth Holcomb had been the key all along. The money could only be a motive after her death. I'm positive Becky's original plan had only included one murder, Elizabeth Holcomb's. That's why Becky started that rumor and why she arranged for an apprenticeship at Lansdale. She wouldn't normally have been in any hurry to dispose of Elizabeth, but if Becky was the attendant with her today and if Becky had seen us at the sanitarium—" I left the rest of the statement unfinished.

"Of course." My wife filled in the blanks. "If your other suppositions were correct, then you were afraid that Becky might panic and get rid of Elizabeth Holcomb right away."

I nodded. "Even though she had already murdered Derek and Lowell, and obviously she didn't know those attempts had been successful, Becky still didn't plan to hurry Elizabeth Holcomb's demise, not until she thought we were getting too close. As a matter of fact, Derek only got killed because he entered the picture unexpectedly."

"You mean Derek was never meant to die?"

I shook my head. "No, I'm not saying that. I'm sure Becky would have gotten around to him sooner or later. Just as she would also eventually have targeted me. Remember, Becky knew about our existence—and our potential threat to her inheritance—from Addie."

"But Becky would still have inherited," Lee protested, "even with you and Derek as co-claimants."

"You're probably right," I admitted. "But the exact terms under which the will is written might have presented her with some problems. If you recall what I told you, the will only refers to Elizabeth Holcomb's children. Or, to be exact, John Holcomb's grandchildren. The lineage ends there, but I'm sure a good lawyer possibly could have made a strong case for Becky as well. However, I don't think she was willing to take that chance."

Lee laughed. "No, that's obvious." Suddenly, her tone turned grim. "So if Derek hadn't stumbled in when he did, Elizabeth Holcomb's death would not have raised any eyebrows. Or, later, neither would Derek's death. Or, much later, yours." Her voice rose half an octave on the last word. "Kyle, you know what that means?"

I nodded. "It means both Derek and Lowell saved my life."

I handed Lee the ferret. "Now do you understand why this little animal is so important to me?"

Lee took Weezer into her arms.

"Yes, it's true," my wife acknowledged, nuzzling Weezer against her cheek. "We do owe a lot to her owners." Lee then held the ferret out in front of her face, just inches from her eyes. Weezer flicked her tongue across the bridge of Lee's nose. My wife laughed.

Suddenly, a loud booming voice reverberated across the room. "What the hell is going on here?"

It was Lieutenant Ricketts.

CHAPTER 22

"Despite the presence
of some oddly appealing
two-footed characters,
it is
nevertheless the four-footed variety
that really steals the
show."

—Stokes Moran, on Lilian Jackson Braun's
The Cat Who Came to Breakfast

*F*our nights later Lee and I finally flew back home to Tipton. In the matter of transporting the ferret, I wasn't certain what problems I might encounter with the airline, so I didn't even take the chance. I just stashed Weezer away in Lowell's parka, and no one was ever the wiser.

Primarily the reason Lee and I had remained in Louisville four extra days was so we could attend the memorial service for Derek and Lowell, as well as the separate funerals for Elizabeth and Becky. Lieutenant Ricketts, once he had calmed down and I had explained everything to his satisfaction, proved to be of enormous help in cutting through the bureaucratic red tape. Derek's body had arrived at the mortuary just two hours before the service was to begin. But then, as I like to say, enough is as good as a feast.

And feast it was, at least for the media, which went on a feeding frenzy. When the story broke the morning following Becky's death, her murderous rampage made national and international headlines—newspapers, television and radio networks, tabloids, anyone out to make a buck capitalized on it in four-inch type. Factor in the Holcomb fortune, the sexual escapades of the principal players both past and present, the celebrity status of the families, and needless to say we had a circus atmosphere surrounding the burials.

Addie attended, of course. Flanked by me on one side and Lee on the other in an effort not only to give her physical support but also to shield her from the media spotlight, Addie somehow found the strength to get through all the public events of the next three days. She even insisted on seeing Lee and me off at the airport this afternoon. As I leaned down to kiss her good-bye, she clutched her arms around my neck and held me tight against her body. As I broke the embrace, I promised I'd see her soon.

Which looks like a promise I will easily keep. I hired the lawyer who provided Lowell with the copy of John Holcomb's will—I fished the envelope out of the trash and found his name on the return address. He tells me I'll have to confer with him a good bit in the coming months while he represents me in the estate settlement. But he doesn't anticipate too protracted a litigation. And he says, conservatively speaking, my inheritance will probably amount to something closely approximating a billion dollars, give or take a few hundred million here or there.

But none of that matters right now. "I'm just glad to be home," I said to Lee our first evening back. "I'm amazed it's still May. It seems like a year since I left."

My wife, lying in bed with several pillows propped behind her back, held a magazine open in her lap.

"Are the animals getting along all right?" she asked drowsily.

I grinned. "As well as can be expected, I guess," I answered, unbuttoning my shirt. "Weezer stole some of Bootsie's food, and now the dog growls every time the ferret comes close."

"Do you think that'll be a problem? Maybe we should keep them apart."

I shook my head. "You know Bootsie. Her bark is always worse than her bite. As soon as Weezer discovers that fact, the little ferret will rule the roost around here, believe me."

Lee smiled. "In case you don't know it, she already does."

I sat down on the edge of the bed, creating a slight wave in the water bed that bounced Lee gently against the backboard, slipped off my shoes, then my socks.

"What great literature are you reading this time?" I asked somewhat sarcastically while unbuckling my pants. "Let me guess. Is it *Vogue?* Or perhaps even *Architectural Digest?*"

"Neither." Lee closed the magazine and held it up for my inspection. "It's *American Baby.* I thought it was about time you had an heir."

Both I and the room faded to black.

ABOUT THE AUTHOR

Neil McGaughey is the author of two previous Stokes Moran mysteries—*Otherwise Known as Murder* and *And Then There Were Ten*, also published by Scribner. He is currently at work on the fourth novel in the series, *Stokes Moran Must Die!*

A member of Mystery Writers of America and Sisters-in-Crime, he currently resides in Florida.